D0592874

· A PROPER WOMAN ·

A PROPER WOMAN

Lillian Beckwith

St. Martin's Press
New York

Library of Congress Cataloging-in-Publication Data

Beckwith, Lillian.
    A proper woman.

    I. Title.
PR6003.E283P7   1987   823'.914   87-4375
ISBN 0-312-00672-1

First published in Great Britain by Century Hutchinson Ltd.

First U.S. Edition

10 9 8 7 6 5 4 3 2 1

The characters in this book
are not those of any living person.

For Grace

VOCABULARY

		Rough Pronounciation
Bandruidh	A witch	Bandroo
Beannachd leat!	Farewell	Byannack let!
Kelpie	A water sprite	Kelpy
Oidhche mhath!	Goodnight!	Oi-she-va!
Tha e breagh!	Good day!	He breeah!
Slainte mhath!	Good health!	Slan-jee-va!
Strupak	A cup of tea and a bite to eat	Stroopak

· A PROPER WOMAN ·

1

When she reached the path that led to the corrie Anna Matheson paused, steadying her quick breathing as she scanned the meandering sheep track up which she had just climbed. Below, the glen, spread with outcrops of bare rock and sad patches of spring-burned heather, looked desolate as it swooped to meet the relatively fertile area of crofting land where the low stone-built houses of the crofters with their assortment of outbuildings ranged themselves in a random way to overlook the bay. Some of the houses were huddled together – the result of crofts having been apportioned into smaller and yet smaller units so as to ensure an equal division of inheritance among a family of sons; others stood in comparative isolation as if proclaiming that for one reason or another their owners had wished to distance themselves from their neighbours. Anna's own home was such a one. Her eyes picked it out and dwelt on it with distaste. A slouch of a house she had always thought it, its walls showing no trace of the regular limewashing which neatened the other homesteads. Stained dark with the neglect of years it looked as if it might, only recently, have heaved itself out from its surround of puddled earth. Rejecting it, she shivered and, pulling her shawl more cosily around her shoulders as a defence against the increasingly restive breeze, let her gaze move slowly over

1

the crofts, their individual boundaries identifiable only by piecemeal earth and stone dykes which themselves straggled uphill until they gave way to the sturdy post-and-wire fence erected by the authorities to separate the cultivated land from the common grazing of the moors. For some seconds her gaze lingered until, as if irresistibly, it was drawn to follow the twisting, flinty road along which, only a few hours earlier, she had witnessed the procession of black-clad mourners solemnly bearing the coffin of her husband on its way to the waiting, newly dug grave.

Anna's face was bleak as she focused on the small burial ground marked only by sparse, deformed trees, hardy survivors of the rectangular plantation of conifers which a former laird had optimistically tried to grow with the intention that they would provide a degree of shelter and seclusion for the graves. But the laird had been a sassenach, a 'come and go man', unfamiliar with the savagery of Hebridean gales. Now the plantation was little more than stunted trunks and denuded branches, leaving the burial ground distinguishable from the encircling moors only by an obsequial greenness which, like a drape of cerecloth, continued to preserve the close-crowded mounds from the invasive tactics of heather and bracken.

Dragging her eyes away from it, Anna became aware that emotion, not exertion, was quickening her breath again and, fearing that even at such a distance so subdued a reaction might be detectable by some hidden observer, she willed herself to take slow, calming breaths. Turning her back on the burial ground, on the crofts and on the houses, she looked up at the tumbled cragginess that edged the skirts of the steeply rising hills. With sudden decision she went forward, carrying on until she reached the corrie, seeking its concealment before she again paused motionless, to stare fixedly ahead in the attitude of one experiencing, or expecting to experience, some kind of revelation. After a few

2

seconds she closed her eyes, and the hand which had been clutching her shawl relaxed, allowing the breeze to lift the shawl from her shoulders and waft it heedlessly to the ground. Through her body ran a strange, ecstatic tremor which, like an injection of some drug, seemed to be loosening the tautness that for so long had clogged her senses. Her chin lifted and, as she peered abstractedly at the shaft of sky above the narrow corrie, her lips, tightened by the cynicism of the years, softened to release a broken sigh.

But there were no tears in Anna's eyes and no weeping in her heart as she yielded herself to the caress of the sweet, wild wind from the hills.

Anna had hated her husband, hated him with a steady yet passionless hatred that had implanted itself all too soon after their marriage. Never at any time had she pretended to any affection for him; nor for that matter had he troubled to pretend the slightest affection for her. Theirs had been, unequivocally, a marriage of pure convenience with no illusions on either side. Given the choice, Anna would have much preferred to have acted as her husband's housekeeper rather than be, even nominally, his wife, but the choice wasn't open to her. They had been imprisoned by the convention that required a man and a woman not related by birth but yet sharing a home to regularize the situation in the eyes of the minister, the neighbours and their God, in that order, by pledging themselves to each other in holy matrimony no matter how spurious their vows might be. Anna had been courageous enough to want to defy convention but her husband had had his own reasons for insisting on marriage, and because at the time there had appeared to be no acceptable alternative she had reluctantly agreed. She had had ten bitter years to regret her capitulation.

Retrieving her shawl, she again draped it around her

3

shoulders, hugging it across her chest as a protection against the strengthening wind. Slowly she began to retrace her footsteps, but at the entrance to the corrie, instead of continuing the descent to the sheep track which would lead her back to her home, she lowered herself onto a lichen-cushioned boulder, well screened from possible observers while providing her with an early glimpse of anyone approaching. Here she sat in statue-like stillness until the breeze, teasing her hair, coaxed several tendrils from beneath the net in which she had tried to capture her unruly bun. She tucked them back but again they broke loose, and at last she exasperatedly tore off the net and, pulling out the pins, unshackled the tawny tresses for the breeze to have its way with them. The resulting coolness on her scalp was almost heady in its effect. She glanced guiltily in the direction of the village. She must remind herself to constrain her hair before she returned. A woman of her age with wildly flowing hair, particularly on the day of her husband's funeral, would lead them to suspect she had gone mad. But not yet would she confine it, she told herself. Not yet, she resolved, and raked her fingers through her still thick hair so that it could blow about even more freely.

After a few minutes she slid down beside the boulder to settle herself more comfortably on a cushion of dry moss and, as she looked out across the grey- and silver-seamed sea towards the sharp-etched islands which prefaced the horizon, it seemed to her that her mind, slowly uncoiling itself from its self-imposed confinement, was beginning to stretch itself, inciting her memory to range back over her life before Black Fergus, and subsequently hate, had entered into it.

Achingly she recalled her childhood home and the serenity and trust that had enfolded it. She saw her mother, the fine skin of her face creased only by gentle smile lines and her eyes invariably lit with affection even when she found it necessary to chide Anna or her young brother Mata over some

4

misdemeanour. She thought of her father whose stern religious beliefs had made him a revered but often intimidating presence, though she had to admit his domination of the household had been upheld more by frequent biblical quotations rather than by harsh words or actions. Her mind's eye formed a vivid picture of the nightly ritual: her father sitting at the kitchen table with the Gaelic Bible open in front of him, his head haloed by the lamplight as he read aloud the chosen chapters. It was these nightly bible readings which from an early age had inured Anna to sitting completely still for long periods at a time, since the slightest tendency to fidget not only earned the culprit a severe look but, because her father had then insisted on reverting to the beginning of the chapter, had also led to an even longer period of submission. Again in the morning they had sat reverently while he had spoken the prayers that unfailingly preceded breakfast. No matter how sleepy-eyed or hungry she or Mata might have been, the rule was inflexible. There could be no hurrying over prayers even when only a few minutes remained before they had to rush off to school. Breakfast could be skimped or even missed altogether. Prayers never.

Theirs had been a repressive childhood though they had not recognized it as such. They had never glimpsed a different way of life; no child of their acquaintance knew more freedom than they. Repression was as much part of their daily life as were the clothes they wore; it hovered over the whole community, constraining to varying degrees every member of it from childhood to old age, curbing every emotion but piety. There was no escape from its hold save by leaving the island altogether.

Continuing to make a series of forays into her memory, she recalled how when she and Mata were younger they had run wild over the moors, their faces almost always crimsoned by the stinging wind, their bare legs tingling from the friction of

5

the spiky heather. The image came so sharply into her mind that it seemed to Anna that the lissomeness of her youth was again coursing through her limbs, giving her the sensation that she could, at that moment, leap up and run as lightly as she had all those years ago. The sensation persisted until she consciously stifled it, telling herself that, though hard work and plain fare had ensured she had retained her slim body and lightness of foot, lissomeness had congealed into a heavy listlessness.

She thought of times when she and Mata had joined the other children of the village for the annual expeditions to collect seagulls' eggs. How agilely they had scrambled and climbed up and across the cliffs to reach the nests; the sound of their excited chattering echoing among the rocks as they compared their success seemed to ring in her ears.

For much of their childhood she and Mata had sought no company but that of each other. Despite Mata being several years her junior they had been good enough companions. Together they had fished for brown trout in the burns and, when the sea was calm, they had fished off the rocks for wrasse and cuddies. Had those hours been as sunlit and pleasant as she now imagined them to have been, she wondered? Had their mother been as pleased as she pretended when they proudly presented her with their catch? On warm summer days they had wandered happily together picking blaeberries and, later, brambles, gorging themselves on the juiciest berries and taking home only the less tempting ones to be made into jam. The cooler days of autumn had brought nutting time when she and Mata had joined with the other children for the long trek to the woods where they had picked the soft, unripe nuts from the trees, filling their pockets with them and eating them until their stomachs were stuffed so full only the long trek back home restored their appetite for food.

Thumbing over the pages of her memory, Anna was

6

reminded that most of her free time had been taken up by croft work. Like all crofter children, as soon as they could be trusted to look after themselves, she and Mata had been required to share in the work of the croft to the limit of their young strength. From an early age they had been allotted simple tasks like feeding the poultry, chasing away marauding sheep and goats and rounding up straying cattle; but as they grew older so had more and more work been expected of them. When it was time for peat digging they had joined in, happily knowing it spelled the end of the gloom and short days of winter. Standing barefoot in the black bog and throwing out the spongy peats as they were cut was a satisfying thing to do, and later, after they had helped with the lifting and stacking of the dry peats, they had helped carry them home, the task developing into a light-hearted contest with other children as to which of them could carry the greater number of peats in their specially woven creels. They had taken their place at the communal potato planting; at haymaking time they had raked and turned and cocked the scythed hay; when the corn was ripe they had worked beside their parents, gathering the cut corn into sheaves which they then tied ready for stooking as soon as the sun had dried them.

As she recalled the work she recalled also the exhaustion after hours of urgency to get the cocks and stooks covered before the threatening rain. She saw her mother's face drawn with fatigue, felt the leadenness of her own young limbs and the overmastering desire for sleep that had followed the long days of toil. And yet she could not recall that either she or Mata had ever voiced a grumble, even to each other. The family had lived mainly off the food the croft produced; the peat they helped bring home cooked that food. Since earliest childhood they had been inculcated with the belief that the croft, along with the health and strength to work and gain a living from it, was a blessing bestowed on them by a

7

beneficent but selective God. One must be proud and grateful to have been chosen to receive such a blessing, and the labour entailed must therefore be regarded as a privilege which, if it could not be wholly enjoyed, must be performed without demur.

2

As soon as she was judged to be old enough it had become one of Anna's duties to go and seek out and report on those of their cows which, not being in milk, were left to graze the open moorland during the summer months. In the early evenings, after she returned from school and had taken her *strupak* and completed her homework, she had enjoyed racing off, skipping barefoot through the heather and singing into the wind as she leaped over rocks and tussocks and waded through peaty pools. Mata, being younger and therefore less fleet of foot, rarely accompanied her on such errands and she was able to revel in the solitariness and freedom of the moors without the frustrations of having to wait for him to catch up with her or having to shepherd him over hazards where he was not so surefooted as herself. Alone she could dawdle, race, climb or leap whenever she fancied, often daring herself to take risks which, had her brother been there, would have brought a rebuke from her mother.

The faintest of smiles now touched Anna's lips as, continuing to rummage among her memories, she recalled how she had been returning home after checking on the cows one evening, when, in a fit of bravado, she had dared herself to leap over a crag of rock which had for a long time been offering itself as a challenge. Pausing to assess it, she saw there was a short, clear run-up to the rock and since she knew it overhung a soft mossy hollow she also knew she could be sure of having a safe landing place. Racing towards it, she accomplished the leap successfully, letting out a short whoop of delight as her feet touched the ground, but as she straightened herself from the crouched position in which she had landed she saw to her horror that she was not alone. She gasped as she found herself confronted by a young man who was a total stranger. Swiftly surmising he must have suddenly stepped forward from the shelter of the crag, she had a scared moment to think that had she made her leap only a yard or so to her right she would almost certainly have landed either on top of him or on top of his rucksack which lay on the ground beside him. She grew hot with embarrassment and, lost for words, could only stand and stare at him in dumb suprise.

'Well!' exclaimed the young man, backing away a few steps in exaggerated astonishment. 'Or maybe I should say, "Well-come!"' Anna remained silent. 'This is a surprise. I was not expecting a visitor and certainly not one who would drop in quite so literally.' He smiled at her disarmingly but, still getting no response, went on, 'Tell me, am I in the presence of a true nymph of the heather? And if not, where on earth did you come from? It must be earth, surely, even though you appeared to drop down from the sky?' Anna took in that his accent was reassuringly Highland but, still nonplussed by the encounter, continued to stare at him. 'Ah, I'm sorry. I see it is I who have given you a fright. You think perhaps it is a ghost you are seeing, is that it?'

Anna shook her head. Had she suspected him of being any kind of supernatural being she would indeed have been frightened out of her wits, but it was all too obvious to her that he was as human as she was herself. After the initial shock there now remained only fluster and confusion at being in his presence. She felt no fear of him. Finding her voice, she said in English, 'I jumped over the crag above you there,' and indicated the rock. Even now she could remember distinctly how she had struggled to keep the pride out of her voice.

Turning, he looked up at the crag. 'My, but that was some jump!' There was admiration in his voice. 'And barefooted too!' His glance swept over her bare feet. 'You were mighty lucky not to have landed on a pebble or a thorn that could have grazed your foot.'

She lifted one foot and then the other, examining them with only cursory interest. 'I have not hurt myself. I am well used to running and jumping crags and I do it more easily in bare feet than when I am wearing boots,' she told him. 'But I would not have tried leaping over the crag had I known there was someone beneath it.' It was the best she could bring herself to offer by way of apology.

'Of course you would not have done so,' he answered, mimicking the stiltedness of her manner. 'But seeing I myself arrived here not more than ten minutes since, I must make my apology for being here.' He slanted a smile at her.

Disconcerted she looked away from him and a slight frown creased and then immediately fled from her brow. Her wide, serious eyes returned to regard him steadily. At first she had assumed the young man to be some kind of tinker but as soon as he had spoken she knew from his voice that he was more educated than any tinker she had met. Her thoughts were occupied with the problem of how she should react to him.

The young man cocked his head on one side and his smile became a teasing grin. 'You are looking at me very solemnly, nymph of the heather,' he accused. 'Very solemnly indeed. Haven't you yet decided whether I am a ghost or maybe a kelpie intent on luring you to your doom?'

'You are no ghost.' She spoke decisively and the birth of a smile touched her lips. 'And,' she continued with archness creeping into her voice, 'I would not expect to see a kelpie so far from the loch.'

11

'So you have convinced yourself that I am an ordinary human being just?' Anna nodded. 'Good,' he said. He raised his eyebrows quizzically then lowered them with an expression of disappointment. 'You looked for a moment as if you might be going to smile at me,' he remarked. 'But I see I was mistaken; I suspect your smiles are precious and you hoard them so they are seen only by very special people.' Crouching down, he began opening his rucksack. 'Shall I guess that the minister might be one of those special people?' he hazarded in a bantering tone.

His remark almost kindled her smile, but though her eyes glinted she bit her lips hard so as to keep them from twitching. 'I would not dare to smile at the minister,' she admitted and bit her lips even harder as an image of the minister's black-garbed figure and cheerless face flitted across her mind.

'You wouldn't?' He looked up at her in mock surprise. 'Are you afraid he might strike you with his Bible if you did? Or preach against you from his pulpit?' He spoke in such a grave voice that the chuckle Anna had been striving to repress burst merrily from her throat. Gaining courage, she said, 'I am thinking you are a stranger in these parts.'

'I am no stranger to the hills and the glens if that is what you are meaning. I was born and brought up as a Highlander in a true Highland home but I no longer belong in that home. Now I belong nowhere. I am a freeman of the hills and glens. A wanderer.' His voice had taken on a kind of chanting note which reminded Anna of the way they recited poetry at school. 'I am a wanderer and I am also a seeker,' he added.

'A seeker?' she interrupted, beginning to suspect he was a follower of one of the curious religious sects, alluded to in a general way as 'pilgrims', who visited the village from time to time.

'A seeker after treasure,' he elucidated, much to her relief.

12

She realized she would have been disappointed if he had turned out to be a 'pilgrim'.

'What like of treasure would you be likely to find hereabouts?' she asked him, hoping he would not say 'Souls.'

'I seek for pearls, nymph of the heather,' and, seeing her puzzlement, he went on, 'pearls of wisdom, perhaps; pearls of true knowledge, shall I say? But no, I am more practical.' Indicating the cleft stick which lay on the ground beside his rucksack, he explained, 'I seek among the mussels in the burns and rivers, and sometimes, if I am lucky, I find a pearl inside one or two of them. You will surely have heard of mussel pearls?' She nodded uncertainly. 'Mussel pearls are almost as pretty as oyster pearls and when I have polished them a little I sell them. And I have not come near to starving yet, though I admit I have needed to take odd jobs at times when pearls are scarce.' Taking out a paper-wrapped parcel from his rucksack and exposing its contents, he held it towards Anna. 'Would you care to share my supper, nymph of the heather, or is it more faery food you are used to?' She declined his offer with a shake of her head. 'No?' He sounded rueful. 'They are sandwiches, hefty sandwiches I admit,' he allowed, holding one of them at arm's length and eyeing it critically, 'but they are wholesome and tasty. They were given to me by the district nurse in a place not a dozen miles from here in return for a wee job I did for her in her garden this morning.' He patted his pocket. 'She also gave me a half crown.'

Anna was disturbed by his candour. Surely an educated man should be ashamed of getting his living in such a beggarly way? Again he proffered the food, and when she again declined he made himself comfortable on the grass and began munching appreciatively.

A tiny drop of rain fell cool on Anna's arm. She looked up at the sky. 'There is a shower coming,' she warned. 'You will

13

need to put up your tent quickly if you are wanting to stay dry.'

'Ach!' He too glanced upwards. 'That is no more than a wee cloud shedding a few tears because it has lost sight of the sun for a whiley. It will soon be finding it again and drying its eyes.' He continued munching, and though she knew it was rude to watch anyone eating Anna lingered, letting the rain soak into her thick hair and dribble down her face. 'I see you do not care about getting wet,' he observed.

'I am well used to it,' she retorted with a shrug of indifference. Putting out her tongue, she licked around her mouth, tasting the rain.

As the young man had predicted, the shower was brief, but in passing it had stolen much of the remaining brightness from the sky. 'Shouldn't you be thinking of running back to your home, nymph of the heather? Or back to your faery dell if that is where you hide yourself?' he suggested. 'Will not your folks be asking themselves if you have been spirited away by the wee folk, or if you have been captured and held against your will by some dreaded human?'

Anna tossed her head. 'They know fine I can take care of myself,' she boasted, but stood up nevertheless, ready to go.

'*Oidhche mhath* then, nymph of the heather,' he called after her.

His use of the Gaelic 'goodnight' so surprised Anna that she stopped in her tracks. So he had the Gaelic! She grew even more curious about him. '*Oidhche mhath!*,' she responded uncertainly and, as she sped homewards, her thoughts were still of the strange young man and the story she would have to tell her parents about her meeting with him.

'What like of a fellow was he?' her father had wanted to know.

'He has fair hair and brown eyes and though he has a beard I am sure he is young because his beard is not thin and stained like old Farquhar's but short and curly like his hair,' she carried on, describing the young man's appearance. 'And his hands and fingernails are not rough and dirty like a tinker's and there was an air about him that I could not understand.' Her detailed observations caused her mother to dart her a searching glance. 'He called himself a "seeker",' Anna resumed, 'And when I asked him what he was seeking for he told me he fishes for mussels in the burns and rivers and that sometimes he is lucky enough to find a pearl inside some of them and this he sells to buy himself food.'

'Ach him!' Her father's tone was so scathing that Anna was startled but she had to wait patiently until he had leisurely attended to the lighting of his pipe before he offered further enlightenment. 'Indeed, I am certainly after hearing of that young man for he's likely the one they call Jimmy Pearl. A sad rebel of a young man he is too. A man that threw away advantages and chances that many another would have given their right arm to have.'

'Aye indeed,' corroborated her mother in a plainly disapproving murmur.

Anna looked from her father's stern face to her mother's troubled one and waited patiently for the story to be continued. 'That young man was born to good, God-fearing parents and brought up in a good, God-fearing home, but didn't he forsake it all to go wandering the roads and glens like a beggar, picking up a living wherever he could,' her father said at last. 'And I doubt the Lord will not forgive him for all the vexation he caused his parents.'

'I was thinking myself he might be a student of some kind,' Anna ventured to say.

'Student!' scoffed her father. 'Student! What like of student is one that turns his back on his education before he's halfway through university?' His tone increased in severity. 'That young man's father is a highly respected schoolmaster and his mother is a daughter of the manse, and from the moment he was born I believe they were set on their son

15

becoming a minister.' Anna tried to imagine the young man wearing clerical garb and with the perpetually dour expression she had learned to associate with ministers. In no way did the image fit.

'I was hearing it near broke his mother's heart when he would have none of the plans she and his father had made for him,' her mother said with a sympathetic sigh. 'Oh, but I'm thinking there must have been some sort of madness in him, surely, to do such a thing.'

'Aye, and I'm told he was a fine scholar and had won many bursaries.' Her father again took up the role of critic. 'They were saying he could have reached a high position in the church. Maybe even have become moderator some day had he not spurned the gifts the Lord had bestowed on him. But he chose to listen to the counsel of the Devil, and no pleas, no threats and no warnings would move him. In the end his father was driven to show him the door and tell him he was not to come back until after he'd mended his wild ways.'

Anna was dismayed. She had been indoctrinated with the belief that the ministry was the most coveted of all the professions. 'Was he very wild?' she asked.

'Is he not living a wild life in the hills?' her father reminded her. 'Have you not now seen that for yourself?'

'How long ago is it since he left his home and went wandering?' her mother queried.

'Close on three years, I would say,' her father replied.

'And will he not have been back to see his parents in all that time?' Anna had been anxious to know.

'If that young man you've seen was Jimmy Pearl then the answer is likely no, he will not have been back. There will be no welcome there for him as I understand it. Not until he has given up his wanderings and come to his senses. His father is a good man but a hard one, they say. He will have meant what he told his son.'

Anna was troubled. Though she supported her parents in

16

condemning the young man's rejection of all his opportunities and the plans his parents had made for him, she was loth to think that someone with such abilities was having to do menial tasks in order to eke out a living. 'When Jimmy Pearl finds a pearl in a mussel and supposing he's able to sell it, will he get good money for it?' she inquired.

'As much as it's worth.' It was her mother who had replied to her question. 'I doubt that, clever as he is, he'll prove to be no loon when it comes to making a bargain. And there's plenty want to buy them. Tourists and even the laird's wife herself is one that's always been keen on the mussel pearls the tinks find. She has a brooch set with them but she says now the tinkers are wanting too much for the pearls and she can no longer afford them. All the same, I'm hearing there's many of her grand friends that's still eager to have them. I daresay he'll do well enough.'

Anna could remember even now how she had gone to bed that night, her head still full of the strange young man. Though she was of her mother's opinion that he must have been mad to have turned his back on his home, his parents and his chances of success, she still hoped he would prosper. She could even remember how she had dared reinforce her hopes by slipping in among her prayers that night a little plea that he might find plenty of mussel pearls.

3

Anna had not expected that Jimmy Pearl would still be there
the following evening but, all the same, curiosity impelled
her steps towards the craggy hollow with the idea of only
peeking to see if there remained any trace of him. She
surprised herself by being oddly pleased to see him crouching
over his camping stove. Instead of concealing her presence she
deliberately let herself be seen.

'*Tha e breagh!*' he greeted her. 'Am I to be honoured once
more with your company, nymph of the heather?'

She hesitated, debating whether or not merely to gesture in
acknowledgement and then continue on her way, but interest
in the young man overcame her indecision. It was with
feigned reluctance that she picked her way down towards the
crag.

'May I offer you a share of my farewell feast?' he invited,
lifting up the frying pan and holding it out towards her. The
hunger-making smell of its sizzling contents wafted over to
her. 'Bacon and black pudding! Does that not strike you as
being food fit for a king?' he asked. Anna swallowed the
sudden relish she had for the food. 'And I have also bread, a
little stale perhaps but crisp when it is fried, and I have tea
though I confess to having only one mug and one dish.' With
his other hand he proffered a steaming mug of black tea.

Anna wrinkled her nose. Even had she fancied the tea she would still have refused it. She dismissed his offer aloofly.

'I will take neither your tea nor your food,' she told him.

'Ah, you are still too proud to share food and drink with a wanderer of the moors,' he challenged with assumed reproach.

'No, indeed I am not,' she was quick to deny. Her blush rose as she went on. 'I would be greedy if I took your food when I have already taken a *strupak* before I left and when there will surely be salt herring and potatoes waiting for me when I get back.' She knelt down beside a clump of heather a few companionable yards away from him.

'Ah, your *strupak!*' There was a tinge of ecstatic remembrance in his voice. 'Tell me now, would I be right in guessing that you have had scones fresh from the girdle and well spread with home-made butter and topped with crowdie so thick that when you bit it you sported a white moustache? Is that not so?'

Anna permitted herself a shy grin. 'Indeed, that is so,' she rejoined. 'And the scones were hot so that the butter melted and ran down my chin and my mother said I had a yellow beard to match my white moustache.' She caught herself pondering why she found him so easy to talk to after so short an acquaintance.

'It is some while since I ate scones fresh from a girdle,' he admitted.

She regarded him soberly. 'Is that not your own fault entirely?' The moment she had put the question she regretted the impulse that had made her do so.

'My own fault entirely,' he agreed. 'But then, how would I find space for a girdle and a basin and such things as milk and flour in my rucksack?'

Convinced in her own mind that he was pretending to have misunderstood the purport of her question, she felt her unease increasing, pushing her into persistence. 'That is not

19

what I was meaning,' she dared herself to say. 'My father told me you chose to turn your back on your home and to throw away your chances of becoming a minister or perhaps a lawyer. He said your home was a good one and your parents greatly respected yet you chose to lead the life of a wanderer.'

He glanced at her with raised eyebrows and then his face set. She wondered if she had angered him.

'Your father told you that, you say?' Anna nodded. Several moments passed before he spoke again and she was relieved to discern no trace of anger in his voice. 'It is quite true what your father has told you.' His admission was followed by a further period of silence. Draining his mug, he flung the dregs on the grass and stared up at the high peaks of the hills, a faraway look in his eyes. Anna waited, occupying herself by plucking at the moss with her fingers. It seemed that the young man had said all he intended to say on the subject but, perceiving the tolerant smile that had settled around his mouth, she became emboldened.

'Why did you do such a stupid thing?' she pursued.

He turned a quizzically amused glance on her. 'You are too young to understand.' His voice was gentle.

'I am not too young to know I could never think of doing such a thing,' she retorted.

'Not even if you knew you were going to be desperately unhappy if you did what everyone had planned for you?'

'How could you have been unhappy?' She was aghast. 'How could that be when you had such clever and respected parents? And when you had such a fine home that had running water that came hot or cold from the taps as you wished and that had a door at the front for visitors and another door at the back? And when you yourself were clever enough to go to university?' He still wore his amused smile. 'All this my parents told me. They said you threw away chances many another would give their right arm to have,' she finished accusingly.

20

The faraway look returned to his eyes as he again lifted his gaze to the hills. 'Yes, indeed, nymph of the heather, I confess I had all that, and to please my parents I did go to university, but I was not happy there and very soon I knew that what I might achieve at university was not what I wanted to achieve. And I decided also that I did not wish to live in a city, which was where the university was and where all universities seem to be.' He shot her a glance. 'Tell me, have you ever visited a city?'

'No,' she admitted. 'But I think I should very much like to. Not yet perhaps but when I am older. I want to become a teacher when I leave school; the schoolmistress says I am clever enough. If I do so, then I would likely need to live in a city.'

'And you think you would like that?' Anna nodded. 'You will not be able to run barefoot in the city as you do here,' he pointed out.

She took his remark as an aspersion. 'Indeed, I would not think of running barefoot when I am grown up and become a teacher,' she reproved him.

'All the same, I think you will not like the city for as long as it takes your father to scythe and gather in his crop of corn. Three Sabbaths in the field, is that not the recognized length of time? Ah, yes, you see, I know a little about work on the land. Three weeks and I think you would be longing to wake again to the calling of curlews and oystercatchers or even the charivari of gull cries rather than the thumping roar of traffic and the noise of hooters and sirens and of bells jangling. You would surely miss the honking of ravens and the mewing of buzzards, the song of the skylarks, the evening drumming of snipe. And your eyes would yearn to see sea stars dancing in the sunshine and sky stars shooting across the darkness.' His own eyes had become dreamy, his voice had taken on a kind of low earnestness that made Anna suspect he had forgotten her presence and was talking to himself.

21

'But you forgot that folks in the cities can wear lighter clothes than we wear. They do not have to clothe themselves against the wind or listen to it trying to take the roof of their house,' Anna reminded him. 'And when there is rain it just drops without the wind driving it, so folks can keep dry by holding an umbrella above their heads,' she added.

'True,' he admitted. 'The wind that blows in the city is sluggish with dust. It cannot blow with any spirit. It does not come fresh from the sea to cool and freshen and buff and polish your skin to the rosy glow I see on your own cheeks. The rain is full of soot, not salt. You would not wish to put out your tongue and taste the rain as I saw you doing last evening.'

She acknowledged his observation with a shy smile. 'All the same, I would like to know what it's like to walk in the rain holding an umbrella over my head,' she confessed. 'And to know that each day will be calm,' she ended wistfully.

'There is no calmness in the city, little nymph of the heather. Everywhere there is noise and argument. As people walk in their hard-soled shoes their feet argue with the pavements; the traffic argues, buses with cars, lorries with trams. Even the buildings, gracious though some of them are, demean themselves by arguing with what little sun manages to peep through the gloom, saying, "You shall not shine here nor there; these places are reserved for our shadows and in the city shadow is more important than sunlight."' He flicked her a quick glance and saw the scepticism of her expression.

'It is true what I am saying,' he insisted. 'But shall I tell you what I think is the worst thing that has happened in the cities?' Without waiting for her reply he went on, 'The worst thing, in my opinion, is that cities have overcome the darkness of the night. There is no true night, no darkness there any more,' he emphasized. 'Always and everywhere there are lights. They shine close about you and they shine in the far distance, reminding you of their presence and of the

22

presence of millions of others who would consider themselves blind without them. I am one who believes that man needs the dark to help soothe the irritations of the day. Not so the city dwellers; they have renounced the benison of true darkness.' His voice became cynical. 'They pay the authorities to provide the light which they then draw their curtains to shut out, whereas I, when I lie in my sleeping bag in the heather, thank my Creator for giving me the coverlet of the dark.'

He stopped speaking and looked directly at her. She was studying him with such a sombre air that his own face creased into a roguish smile. 'You think I am talking nonsense, do you not?'

'Yes, indeed I do,' she responded unflinchingly. He threw back his head and laughed. 'I do not much care for the dark,' Anna explained.

'Are you telling me you do not like to see the sky ablaze with shimmering stars and the moon lit by silver as it rises above the black hills?' he chaffed. 'You would not see such things if there were no longer darkness.'

She turned her head away, unsure as to whether or not she should encourage him to continue with his strange talk. Listening to him had the effect of muddling her own thoughts. She said decisively, 'If you had stayed at the university my father says you would surely have achieved a proud position in life. Instead you are a wanderer known as Jimmy Pearl. Did you know that is the name people have for you?' she taxed him.

He chuckled as he put out the primus and set the frying pan on the grass. 'And should I not be proud to be known as Jimmy Pearl?' he demanded. 'I am happier than many of the people I meet. I owe nothing, I cheat no one. I take nothing that is not given freely in return for my labour, and yet here I am, free to go or stay as I please. I remain my own master.' The tiny smile that had wanted to trace itself around Anna's mouth in sympathy with his laughter vanished. Her lips pursed disapprovingly.

'And now,' he nodded towards the hills where the sun was preparing to hide itself behind the first of the stark peaks, 'I am happy and I intend to eat my supper while there is still light to see what I am eating. No more questions. I myself have talked too much and kept you back from completing your errand. It is high time you were away to your home, nymph of the heather.' His tone was plainly dismissive.

She rose. 'One more question,' she pleaded. 'Why do you call me nymph of the heather?'

He looked surprised. 'Do you not care to be called by that name?'

'It sounds foolish.' She tried to make her voice sound haughty.

'Very well, I will tell you.' He held up one hand, spreading out the strong, straight fingers as he counted off his reasons. 'Firstly, it is because you are a beautiful young maiden and poets and writers almost always describe such maidens as "nymphs", particularly so when they have hair like yours which is the colour of autumn bracken when the sun is on it. Second, it is because when you left me last evening to run home your little white heels went twinkling through the heather as if you were a fairy scattering silver charms behind you as you ran. And, thirdly,' he added with a faint rebuke, 'it is because you have not deigned to tell me you have a name at all.'

'My name is Anna,' she told him primly. 'Anna Matheson.' She turned to go but, looking back, called over her shoulder. 'You spoke of this being your farewell feast. Does that mean you will not be here tomorrow?'

An elaborate shrug of the shoulders was his only response. He put a forkful of black pudding into his mouth.

'I was thinking if I was sure you would still be here tomorrow I would bring you some fresh girdle scones and

24

some of my mother's butter and crowdie,' she offered.

He grinned and clicked his tongue appreciatively. 'I will be here,' he assured her.

The next evening, wanting him to have the scones while they were still warm from the girdle, she had taken the food to him on her way out to the cattle, leaving him to enjoy them in her absence. When she returned she found him sitting with his back against the rock, his arms hugging his hunched knees. He was so still that, thinking he might be asleep, she approached him stealthily, mischievously intent on waking him with a sudden shout. Her plan was thwarted by his called greeting.

'That was good indeed,' he enthused. 'I am grateful to you and your mother for providing me with such a feast. Say to your mother that Jimmy Pearl believes she makes the best girdle scones and butter and crowdie he has ever tasted. The best in the whole world maybe.'

'Ach, they were nothing,' Anna deprecated. She knelt down on the grass, perfectly at ease with him and eager to listen to what he might have to say. She wondered if he would return to the subject of his days in the city but instead he questioned her about her school and her teacher, about the lessons she enjoyed most, about the kind of books she liked to read. Changing her position, she noticed the dampening grass against her bare legs and at the same time became aware of an increasing chill in the air. Looking out to sea, she saw how the mist which had 'formed over the horizon was now creeping inexorably towards the land. She had no liking for being out on the moors in the mist. It had the effect of making the familiar seem strange to the point of eeriness. She jumped up. 'I must go,' she declared. 'The mist will be down soon.'

'Indeed, so it will,' he agreed casually, following her glance. 'But since you are unlikely to see me again around these parts I should like you to take this with you.' Putting

25

his hand inside his jacket, he took out a matchbox and held it out on the palm of his hand.

Anna put her hands behind her back. 'Why would you be wanting to give me a box of matches?' she asked suspiciously. 'I have no need of such a thing.'

'Take it and open it if you will, and you will find it is not a box of matches. It is my farewell gift to a beautiful and kind and clever young maiden,' he explained.

She took the proffered box and, cautiously sliding it open, saw it contained two small pearls resting on a tiny cushion of fresh green moss. For a moment or two she stared at them. 'For me? To keep?' she breathed, too shy to meet his look.

He nodded. 'Part of the fruits of my labours,' he said.

'Oh, but it is too good of you!' she exclaimed, copying the expression she had heard her mother use on being presented with an unexpected gift. 'They are much too pretty to be given to someone like me,' she said, and added shrewdly, 'You could sell such pretty things, surely?'

He ignored her question. 'You like them?' he asked, and was answered by the glow of her smile. Guessing that she was unaccustomed to receiving presents and therefore had little experience of how to express her gratitude, he said, 'You must not try to thank me now, but when you are grown up and have become a schoolteacher as you so much desire to be, then maybe you will have the pearls set into a brooch or perhaps a pair of earrings which, when you wear them, supposing you ever become sophisticated enough to wear such baubles, will remind you of your meeting with Jimmy Pearl and of how you listened so patiently to the nonsense he talked. That will be all the thanks I shall want.'

'But you will not be here for me to thank you then,' she said.

'Who knows what the future may bring?' he teased.

She slid the matchbox shut and gripped it tightly in her hand. 'You will be away on your travels soon, then?' She

26

allowed no tinge of regret to affect her tone.

'At first light,' he confirmed. 'With my rucksack on my back I shall hie me off to pastures new. So it is *Beannachd leat*, nymph of the heather. And hurry you home on your swift, light feet before the mist encircles you. It is coming in with such menace now that I fear it may be intent on doing that.'

Again it took her by surprise that he should use the Gaelic language for his farewell. '*Beannachd leat!*' she called and raced homeward. She did not see him again.

She was dubious about showing the pearls to her mother but, uneasy at the thought of secrecy between them, she decided to do so.

'My, my! but that was awful kind of him,' her mother commented. 'No doubt it was his way of saying thank you for the food you took him.'

'The pearls should be yours rightly,' Anna said. 'It was you who made the scones and butter and crowdie, and the young man said I was tell you they were the best he's ever tasted.'

'He sounds still to be the gentleman he was brought up to be,' observed her mother. 'But as for the pearls, I am too old to think of decorating myself with such things. And well you know what your father would say to me if I should do so. No, no. The pearls are yours. Keep them until you are old enough to decide for yourself what you might wish to do with them.'

Anna asked timorously, 'Will I show them to my father?' She waited tensely for her mother's reply.

'Since they are a gift given with every good intention and seeing they are too pretty to be thrown at the back of the fire, I believe you would do well to keep them hidden from all eyes but your own,' her mother advised. 'Men do not always understand such things.' They exchanged a look of complete accord.

Anna was relieved. She had dreaded having to show the

pearls to her father, fearing, as her mother had hinted, that he would immediately command her to rid herself of such baubles by throwing them at the back of the fire. She secreted the matchbox at the bottom of her clothes chest, taking it out and inspecting its contents only when she could be certain of not being observed. But, with the insouciance of adolescence, interest in the pearls had waned as the years went by, as had her interest in the young man who had given them to her. Nurtured as she had always been in the doctrine that scholarship and entry into one of the high professions were to be revered above all other attributes, she had found it easy enough to dismiss the memory of Jimmy Pearl from her mind, and for most of the time the pearls lay undisturbed. Only in the spring during the annual sorting of her clothes chest when it was necessary for every garment to be shaken and hung out in the sun to combat the threat of moths did she have the small pleasure of rediscovering the matchbox. And only then were her thoughts jolted briefly to the now misty image of Jimmy Pearl with his foolish-sounding talk. And if a reminiscent smile momentarily touched her lips, it was invariably succeeded by a disapproving shake of her head over the memory of the young man who, she remained convinced, had been resolved on making such a sad waste of his talents.

4

Anna never achieved her ambition to become a schoolteacher. Her scholastic attainments had earned her commendation and won her bursaries which would have paid for her further education, but the illness and subsequent death of her father, followed by the declining health of her mother, had necessitated her remaining at home during the vital years when she should have been going to college. When her mother had died Anna was twenty-one years old and Mata seventeen. Resigning herself to the knowledge that she was now too old to take up her bursaries and study for a career as a teacher, and convinced that Mata was not yet mature enough to cope on his own, she had accepted the inveteracy of the role imposed upon her. As a daughter of the croft, custom decreed it was her duty to forgo any aspirations of her own so as to ensure the wellbeing of her brother and the upkeep of the croft. Only if her brother took a wife would she have the choice of whether or not she should stay.

It had not been easy to come to terms with what she regarded as her obligations. Though the pull of the croft was strong enough to gentle her resentment, she was at times conscious of an emptiness in her life – a feeling of dissatisfaction with her role. There were periods of frustration when the longing to stretch herself mentally almost consumed her, only to give way before the more urgent demands of physical labour; there were periods of sharp regret when missed opportunities persisted in rearing their images in her mind. But, as far as she could, she assuaged her repining with the books sent to her regularly by a retired schoolmistress whom she had met whilst the latter was on holiday in the village. The long winter evenings, which made Mata so disconsolate, were for her deliverance from the days of toil. She read avidly, letting herself be drawn into the lives of people and into situations the like of which she had never, nor would ever be likely to encounter.

For several years, despite Mata's increasing discontent with the crofting life, they had shared with only minor frictions the work of the croft, dividing on each rent day any small financial gain the croft had made during the year, but Anna could not help noticing that Mata was becoming steadily more morose in his manner even towards her. Suspecting he could be contemplating taking a wife, she cast about in her mind as to which of the village girls he would be most likely to favour, with which of them she would most like to share her home. But, so far as she could perceive, Mata appeared to single out no particular girl for his attentions. She grew puzzled. He was handsome, and though he tended to be lazy she herself saw that the croft was well looked after, so surely any girl would be glad to have him for a husband? She risked alluding to the subject of marriage and tried to chaff him into an admission of a preference, but he responded only by making disparaging comments on every name she mentioned. He began to speak of making a trip to Glasgow where, in his youth, he had once spent a week's holiday, and at last Anna, driven to exasperation by his constant criticism of their way of life, and thinking that a spell in the city would help him to be more appreciative of what the croft had to offer, urged him to go, even to the point of offering to help him with the expense of his journey. So long as he chose a less busy time of the year when there was no peat cutting, no planting, no sheep dipping and no harvest, she could, she assured him, cope with the croft on her own. His eagerness to be persuaded to go had not surprised her, but when, at the end of his three-week holiday, he had returned bringing with him a city girl whom he proudly introduced as his wife, she had been totally dumbfounded.

Politeness disguised Anna's initial shock and disapproval but, resolving she must do her best to make Jeannie, her new sister-in-law, feel welcome, she quickly planned an 'after-wedding' party to which all the neighbours came. The festivities continued all night and intermittently for the next couple of days and Jeannie seemed overjoyed at being the centre of attention. Mata praised her efforts with an enthusiasm that had become rare in him and Anna allowed herself to feel reassured. Doubtless Mata would be less discontented now that he had a wife beside him; more willing to do his share of the work and thus give them a chance to earn substantially more from the croft. She doubted if Jeannie would be strong enough for outside work but she was quick to see the advantages of having another woman in the home. Croftwork was demanding, pushing her sometimes to the limits of exhaustion, and it would be good to come indoors and find a meal ready or in preparation. But it was not only the extra help in the house she could look forward to. Except for Mata and hurried visits to or from neighbours, her life had been virtually companionless. Now there would be someone other than Mata to talk with, and surely Jeannie, coming from the city, would have so much to talk about? The prospect seemed a not unpleasant one and Anna, anticipating that with her help and guidance Jeannie would eventually adapt happily to her new life, genuinely believed that, given time, a true sisterly relationship would develop between them. At no time did it cross her mind that she herself would come to be regarded as superfluous; that she would no longer be expected to continue living in the family home. In crofting communities the right of a son to inherit the croft was regarded as sacrosanct, but at the same time it was an unchallengeable custom that the family home remained as such – a dwelling where ungrudging shelter must be provided for as long as it was wanted for anyone born and bred under its roof. Equally it was an accepted premise that any incomer to that home – be it a needy relative or even a new bride – must merge into the set pattern of the household and make no attempt to introduce unfamiliar ways of her own.

But Jeannie lost no time in making it clear that she had no respect for crofting traditions. Within weeks of her arrival she had begun, in her assertive Glaswegian voice, to criticize, rearrange and insinuate her own ways. Unwillingly she had to acknowledge that since Mata relied on Anna's assistance on the croft – assistance which Jeannie herself was neither qualified nor prepared to offer – she had no alternative to enduring her sister-in-law's presence, but she made no secret of the fact that she resented having to do so.

Anna was at first bewildered by Jeannie's attitude. Surely, she reasoned, when a stranger comes into a family she should try to adjust to the established ways of that family? Only gradually did she come to realize that, far from having to welcome Jeannie into her home, it was she who must now yield authority to the stranger. She struggled to be forbearing, telling herself that she must be patient and let time sort out their relative positions; that Jeannie was no doubt finding it more difficult than she had expected to fit into the quiet pattern of island life after the bustle of the city; that her sister-in-law was young and impetuous; that her lack of interest in the croft and the countryside was due to a lack of understanding.

She tried to coax Jeannie to accompany her when she went out to the moors to milk the cattle, thinking that if she

32

pointed out to her some of the wild creatures she encountered, the impressive rock formations, the clarity of the tumbling burns and the fish darting in the quiet pools, Jeannie would soon become captivated by her surroundings. But Jeannie would not be tempted. She occasionally strolled as far as the shore, only to complain loudly about the steepness of the path; she once or twice poked her head into the byre to observe the cattle, only to retire with a sniff of disgust. Even in fine weather she seemed to prefer to be indoors rather than out and spent most of her time flicking through mail-order catalogues and out-of-date magazines and newspapers.

Anna, still trying to excuse her sister-in-law, thought it would be different when Jeannie was with child. A child in her womb would surely give her a new interest, mellowing her attitude and making her less prickly in her behaviour. She hoped fervently the event would not be too long delayed. But the months went by and Anna could discern no symptom of Jeannie being pregnant. Far from diminishing, her sister-in-law's resentment tended to flare more frequently into open hostility, and as Anna's capacity for tolerance shrank she returned to speculating, as she had on first meeting Jeannie, as to why Mata had chosen a wife who, though vivacious and undeniably pretty in what she privately thought of as a 'town pavement' kind of way, was so patently unsuited for life on an island where movement was limited by tides; where communications were often disrupted by storms; where she could find none of the amenities and entertainments to which she had been conditioned; and where she would come into contact with a Sabbath that was so strictly observed it must seem to her that even before the day was allowed to dawn it was enveloped in a black shroud of piety too oppressive for so much as a raised voice to be permissible. Anna wondered why Jeannie had agreed to marry Mata and come and live on the croft. Had Mata not painted a true picture of what she must expect? On the other hand, was Mata so handsome that she found him irresistible?

Not wishing to be the target of Jeannie's petulance, and irritated beyond bearing by her brother's phlegmatic indifference to the strained atmosphere of the kitchen, Anna tried to efface herself whenever possible, forsaking the fireside at night for the chill privacy of her bedroom. It was a small room with little space for movement. That, she had always lived with, but since Jeannie had been lured by one of the mail-order catalogues into buying new furniture for her and Mata's room and had then moved the old furniture into Anna's room, the space had become even more confined. Not wishing to see her parent's possessions chopped up for firewood or banished to the byre, Anna had made no protest, though she could no longer open her clothes chest without first transferring most of her books onto the bed and could not sit on the one chair there was space for without first moving her lamp onto the floor. Every day she found herself having to fight her rising bitterness not only against Jeannie but against her bother. She began to despise Mata for his submissiveness to his wife's incessant demands for improvements to the house. As soon as the weather took on an edge of coldness Jeannie, complaining that the cottage, which Anna had always found warm and cosy, was unendurably cold and uncomfortable, insisted on replenishing the fire so frequently that Anna, seeing how quickly the stack of peats was dwindling, remonstrated in Mata's presence, pointing out that the stack was meant to last them though the winter. Mata immediately ordered a delivery of coal – the first that had ever 'disgraced' the cottage, as her father would have said. Soon the peat reek, which had steeped itself into the memory as it had into the very fabric of the walls of the cottage, was overlaid by the coarse smell of coal smoke, which, so it seemed to Anna, repulsed rather than welcomed her into the kitchen.

The following spring the old iron range had to be thrown out and replaced by a shiny, modern grate; a brightly patterned wallpaper was pasted over the varnished, peat-stained wood that lined the walls. A new kitchen table and chairs were bought to replace those which her father had fashioned from driftwood and which had stood sturdily ever since she could remember in the centre of the room and within handy reach of the range. The oatmeal and flour girnels were removed from their places on either side of the fireplace and relegated to the barn where, being at the mercy of the damp and the mice, their contents more often had to be fed to the poultry rather than be used for human consumption. Jeannie's extravagances continued to grow and Anna winced every time she entered the kitchen and found her sister-in-law poring over the innumerable mail-order catalogues from which she ordered so recklessly.

By the time the second spring of Jeannie's residence at the cottage came round Anna had begun to dread the annual visit of Tina-Willy, the old tinker woman who regularly toted her bundle of apparel and household linen from croft to croft. In the village Tina-Willy had always been accepted as one of the harbingers of spring and every household willingly purchased from her bundle in the hope of being regaled with news and chat about the goings-on of other villages which, though they might have kin there, they rarely had the chance to visit. However, it was seldom that the annual transaction ran to more than two or at the most three items per family, the crofters shrewdly suspecting that to buy more would encourage Tina-Willy to become more emphatically im-portunate on subsequent visits. But Jeannie knew no such reservations. She bought from the old tinker with such eagerness that the normally stolid Tina-Willy could barely hide her astonishment. Anna suspected she was wishing she had asked twice the price for her goods.

With mounting despair Anna pleaded with Mata to try to

35

reason with his wife. 'How can you afford to indulge her, Mata?' she asked.

'That's my business,' he answered shortly.

'And mine, Mata,' she reminded him.

He was obviously disturbed by her question but explained, 'Jeannie's used to better things. She cannot live the way we're used to and I do not expect her to.'

The following week he had to send off some of their best stock to the sale so as to foot the bills for Jeannie's lavish spending, and though she did not remonstrate with him she knew from his worried expression that, like herself, he had begun to fret over their future livelihood.

Jeannie's spending became the talk of the village. 'Mata must have found a sack of money when he was out fishing,' they jested, and Anna, echoing Mata's defence, returned loyally, 'Jeannie cannot be expected to be content with old things. She's young and likes brightness around her. She will take a while to settle herself.'

'A bairn would settle her,' they said. 'What's Mata about that he has not given her a bairn yet? Is he not "all correct", as they say of the bulls here?'

Anna grinned weakly. 'Right enough, a bairn will settle her,' she agreed.

But as time went by it seemed to Anna that Jeannie, instead of showing a willingness to settle, grew more restless and peevish. With strained generosity she continued to attribute her sister-in-law's moods to the fact that she had now been married to Mata for more than two years and as yet she was showing no signs of pregnancy. It was understandable that a woman in such a situation must be troubled, thought Anna, whose view was that children were the desired fulfilment of marriage and could never come too soon. A few weeks later she thought she detected a renewed animation about Jeannie, a noticeable rekindling of the sparkle in her eyes. Anna's own spirits lifted as she hoped she guessed the reason for it. Surely if there was now to be a child there would be more accord between her sister-in-law and herself? More contentment in the home? She began trying to evade Jeannie less than she had been used to doing, giving her sister-in-law an opportunity to make her announcement, but Jeannie was not forthcoming and Anna would not appeal to her directly.

On her way out to the hill for the milking one evening she heard Mata hammering in the byre and, since there had of late been so few occasions when she could speak to him away from Jeannie's hearing, she changed course and went over to the byre. Mata was mending one of the cow stalls. He looked up as she entered.

'Oh, just hold on to this for me while I get these nails in,' he told her. She stood beside him, holding the support until it was fastened. 'That'll do for a time,' he said, testing its firmness.

'It needed doing,' she said.

'There's a lot needs doing to this place,' he admitted disconsolately, and looked up at the sagging beams that supported the thatched roof.

'There's plenty of good wood down at the shore for sorting it when you have time,' she pointed out. 'It'll need the two of us.'

'Ach!' He shrugged his shoulders and threw the heavy hammer into the waiting wheelbarrow. He gripped the handles and made to go.

'I'm noticing Jeannie seems to be happier in herself lately,' she ventured tentatively.

'Aye,' Mata agreed. He began to trundle the wheelbarrow away. 'That's because she's at last getting what she's long been wanting,' he called over his shoulder. A smile spread itself over Anna's face.

The suspicion that Jeannie was with child had immediately aroused Anna's own thwarted maternal instincts and, coming back from the hill, she wondered how long she would have to wait before Jeannie confided she was pregnant. She hoped Jeannie would not keep her secret too long for surely the sooner they shared the knowledge the sooner the feeling between them could begin to grow warmer. As she approached the cottage she heard Jeannie singing. The sound confirmed her suspicions and as she opened the door into the kitchen she looked at her sister-in-law with a new tenderness. She was totally unprepared for Jeannie's exuberant greeting.

'Well, and what have you to say now you know about us going back to live in Glasgow?' Jeannie demanded.

Anna blinked in surprise. 'Live in Glasgow?' she exclaimed. 'Who's going to live in Glasgow? What nonsense is this you have got hold of?'

'D'you mean Mata hasn't told you?'

'Mata has told me nothing.'

'Oh, I was sure he must have when I saw you were with him in the byre before you went out to the hill.' Anna stared at her. 'It's not nonsense,' Jeannie assured her. 'Me and Mata are going to live in Glasgow. My dad's got Mata a good job to go to.' Jeannie spoke with such an air of confidence that Anna was forced to believe there must be some truth in what she was saying.

'My brother is surely not the kind of man who would want to leave his croft and go to work in Glasgow,' she objected, trying to ignore a sudden claw of doubt.

'You don't know your brother as well as I do then and that shouldn't surprise you,' Jeannie retaliated. 'Mata's not like you. He's not content to rot here on the croft in this backward place. He's bored. Anybody but yourself could see that. He wants to be somewhere he can go for a bit of pleasure when he's done with work of an evening.' Anna was about to interrupt but Jeannie carried on. 'Anyway, Mata

38

thinks more of my happiness than he thinks of what you and your grandfather and great grandfather would have wanted,' she gloated. 'So, it's all cut and dried. My dad's got him this job and we've the promise of a nice flat not far from the shops and with a bit of green that will keep him happy. Oh,' Jeannie stretched her arms above her head in a gesture of exultation, 'I'm so thrilled about it I feel I can hardly wait. I really can't.'

'But Mata will never be happy there. He knows almost nothing of city ways.'

'He knows well enough where he wants to live. And if he finds it a bit strange to begin with he'll soon get used to it,' Jeannie predicted. 'It's not as if he'll be the first man to have exchanged the country for the town and thrived on it.' She treated Anna to a smile of supreme confidence.

Anna eyed her sister-in-law dubiously and a long-ago recollection of Jimmy Pearl's description of life in the city tugged at her memory. She had visited cities since those days. She knew they had to be endured if one was to be successful in a career and the knowledge had affected her with a disproportionate sense of relief when she had decided to stay on the croft after her mother died. But Mata? Mata would never qualify for a career. He was too lazy, too feckless. He would allow himself to be pushed into being a labourer or a factory worker, a job which might provide the money to pay for Jeannie's extravagances but would never compensate him for the freedom he enjoyed now. 'You say you and Mata are definitely going to live in Glasgow?' Jeannie nodded. 'For how long do you propose to stay there?'

Jeannie laughed. 'For ever, of course.'

'What then is going to happen here? Am I expected to work the croft without help?' She thought she would always remember the glint of triumph that lit Jeannie's eyes.

'I've got more news for you, Anna.' Now, when it was too

late for mutual rejoicing, Anna thought Jeannie was going to tell her about the baby, but she was wrong. 'Mata's managed to sell the croft and house.'

'Sold the croft and house?' As if the breath had been knocked out of her Anna could manage only a thin querulous whisper. It was unthinkable that what Jeannie was saying could be true. Inconceivable that a brother should sell the home which was part of her birthright. The croft had been the family's homestead for generations. How could Mata have disposed of it so secretly and with such callous indifference to her circumstances? As she gaped open-mouthed at her sister-in-law Anna felt as if every nerve in her body had been lashed to rawness.

'That's right, sold, *sold*,' Jeannie stressed. 'And for good money too. It is Mata's to sell, you must know,' she reminded Anna and, seeing the way Anna's hand went nervously to her throat, her mouth set implacably as if ready to rebut any plea.

But Anna could not speak. Her sister-in-law's announcement had so wounded and perplexed her that she felt too stunned to grasp fully the import of what Jeannie had said.

'That elderly couple that came here last autumn,' Jeannie elucidated, filling the silence between them. 'Oh, I know I made out to you that they were relatives of my family,' she confessed in response to Anna's questioning frown. 'There was no point in telling you the truth then and upsetting you when it might have come to nothing. Anyway, if you'd known you would have set yourself to persuading Mata against the idea.' Jeannie's glance challenged her. 'Well, this couple were looking out for a place they could buy for their daughter and her husband. They're thinking of setting up a sort of place where they make things to sell to tourists. Kind of craftworks, they said. This place suited them and, believe it or not, all the papers are signed and finished with. There's no chance of any of us going back on anything now, so it's

40

too late for you to try altering Mata's mind.' She threw out her arms ecstatically. 'Oh, it's wonderful. Just three more months and I'll be out of this hole and coming alive again.'

With her right hand Anna lifted the full milk pail that was slung over her left arm and set it carefully on the table. Turning to face her sister-in-law, she asked quietly, 'What is to become of me? Have neither you nor Mata thought about that?'

'God! You're twenty-eight past. You're surely old enough to look after yourself by now,' Jeannie snapped. Not until that moment had Anna suspected just how selfish Jeannie could be, how deep was her sister-in-law's antipathy.

'But this is my home. It has always been my home.' Her voice almost broke as she spoke the words.

'Oh, there's bound to be someone who'll give you a home if you want one.' Jeannie attempted to comfort her. 'After all, this place is full of cousins and aunts, isn't it? You're such an inter-married lot, you're related to almost everyone in the village, aren't you? And you're a good worker. Everyone says that,' she conceded. 'Mata himself has told me there's no one better at working with animals than yourself.' As if it were an afterthought she added, 'You'll have no need to worry about having a roof over your head for as long as you want it. Mata says he's sure of that. He wouldn't have been so eager to sell the place if he hadn't believed that,' she finished in a tone that was meant to be conciliatory.

There followed a long interval of silence while Anna methodically sieved the milk and rinsed out the pails. As if the silence had become accusatory Jeannie burst out, 'Anyway, we can't take you with us, that's sure enough. For one thing the flat we're getting is too small and for another Mata won't be earning enough to provide a free home for you. To start with it's going to be a tight squeeze to look after ourselves. If you were with us you would have to get a job, and let's face it, Anna, you'd look a bit of a frump among city

41

folk, and at your age and with the disadvantage of that crippled arm of yours,' she directed a meaning glance at Anna's left arm, 'well, I doubt if you'd find it so easy, would you?'

Anna gripped her left arm as if protecting it from the impact of Jeannie's cruel reflection. For a second she had to close her eyes to hide the hurt she suspected might be revealed in them. Every word Jeannie had uttered had stung her sharply but she made herself look straight at her sister-in-law and when she spoke there as a shaky pride in her voice. 'My arm may be crippled, as you point out, but it is by no means useless. It has never prevented me from doing what I have a mind to do. Indeed, I believe I make more use of it than many who have two good arms,' she told her cuttingly, 'and I should remind you that work on the land and with animals is not my only talent. I have brains too and had I not stayed to nurse first my father and then my mother I should no doubt have become a schoolteacher.'

'Mmm,' Jeannie admitted, 'Mata told me about that. It's a pity it's too late for you to take that up again, isn't it? Your arm wouldn't have been a drawback there, would it?'

A fit of trembling crept over Anna and she was glad to bend down and pick up the empty peat basket ready to take it out to the stack for refilling. At the door she stopped, panting a little and holding onto the door jamb for support. Looking back over her shoulder at her sister-in-law, she said with as much testiness as she could infuse in her voice, 'If it is of any comfort to you, I may tell you I have no wish to live in Glasgow, neither with you and Mata nor with anyone else for that matter. All I want – all I need and have been led to expect – is that I should be able to stay here in the home I have lived in and have worked for since I was old enough to throw a few handfuls of corn to the hens.'

'I'm sorry Anna, honestly, that it's come as such a blow to you,' Jeannie said with faint contrition. 'But if we'd told you

42

earlier we're sure you would have argued and protested and made the decision even harder for Mata to make.'

I should indeed have argued, Anna reflected, but what chance should I have stood against you?

'Its different for you,' Jeannie resumed. 'You're used to paddling around in clumsy great boots and you don't miss not going anywhere because there's never been anywhere to go. Mata and I are young still and we want to do things while we're young enough to·enjoy them. I feel buried here.' She paused long enough to scrutinize Anna's expression. 'I believe it might do you good to get away from this place and see a bit of life, Anna. Just working and reading is not good for anyone. We might seem to be cruel to you now but the day will come when you'll have cause to thank us for giving you a good shake-up. It's time you faced up to other things. You're too content, Anna. Too content altogether.'

Anna retorted stiffly, 'I faced up to things, as you like to call it, when I chose to give up my chance of becoming a schoolteacher. Let me tell you, it's not easy to throw away the chance of a promising career but as I saw it then I was needed here on the croft. As I see it now, the situation is reversed. It's now I who need the croft.'

'It's too late,' she heard Jeannie call as she went outside.

At the peat stack she took her time filling the basket and just as she was about to hoist it onto her back so as to carry it into the kitchen she saw Mata enter the byre. Deciding that the moment for confrontation had come, she left the full basket leaning against the stack and followed him into the byre. 'Mata?' she called, standing in the open doorway.

Mata had seen her at the stack and had guessed she was likely to follow him. Though his back was towards her he had noticed her shadow temporarily blot out the shaft of light as she entered. 'Aye,' he replied in a muffled voice. As she came towards him he saw her face drained of its usual colour and he knew instantly that Jeannie had not only

43

broken the news he himself had dreaded having to break to her but that she had not been gentle in doing so.

'Mata, is it true?' she pleaded. 'Jeannie tells me you're going to live in Glasgow. That you've sold our home to strangers. I cannot bring myself to believe it but Jeannie swears it's true. Is it, Mata? I want to hear it from your own lips.' Her eyes beseeched him.

His own eyes slid away and he felt his throat dry up at the note of pain and accusation in her voice. Above the unbuttoned neck of his shirt the muscles of his throat worked as he tried to swallow the dryness.

'Aye, it's true, Anna,' he admitted in a taut thick voice. In the dim light of the byre his weathered outdoor face looked drawn and as he was about to throw a forkful of hay into the rack his shoulders sagged. Lowering the hay to the floor, he leaned on the fork as if the strength had suddenly gone out of him.

'But how can you have been persuaded to do such a thing, Mata? It is not like you. It is underhand and deceitful. This is our home. Yours and mine. We belong here and nowhere else. Our roots are here as are the roots of our ancestors. We are as much part of this place as are the crags and the lochans, the heather and the hills. Here we have security,' she cried, her voice rising with the vehemence of her entreaty. 'Will you have such security in a flat in Glasgow?'

Mata turned away, giving his attention once more to forking up the hay. 'Don't think I'm not feeling bad about it, Anna. I am, but that's the way it had to be. The croft's got to be sacrificed,' he said dully. 'Jeannie will never settle here, she hates it too much.'

'Jeannie!' she flung the name at him scornfully. 'How could you be so weak, Mata?' Knowing it would only alienate him she bit back the rest of what she wanted to tell him: that he was a fool ever to have married Jeannie and to have imagined she would ever take to the crofting life.

44

Instead she asked, 'Do you think you will be happy in Glasgow, Mata?'

'Aye, I'm thinking I might be,' he mumbled. 'Happier than I'd be staying here without Jeannie.'

His shame was so apparent, his voice sounding so near the edge of breaking that Anna felt a sudden rush of tenderness towards him. He was, after all, her brother, the young brother she had watched over and encouraged. Mata had never been as strong-willed as herself; where she had been venturous he had been timid, and now, obviously besotted with Jeannie, he was allowing her to mould his life for him. He's bound to get homesick, Anna told herself. A couple of years in Glasgow at the most and he'll be wanting back here.

'There's no need to sell the croft though, is there, Mata?' she pressed. 'Surely it's not too late to change your mind about that? I could carry on here on my own if we got rid of some of the cattle and sheep, and then you would always have your home to come back to. Wouldn't it comfort you to know that there would be this safe anchorage waiting for you?' It was persuasion rather than reasoning she was attempting now. 'It would have been the way our mother and our father would have wanted it. They would never...'

He cut her short. 'It's sold,' he said. 'There's no going back on it now so let there be an end to your girning.' He dug the fork savagely into another load of hay and flung it up into the rack. Anna did not move. He continued throwing forkful after forkful of hay and still she stood watching him, crushed by the hostility of his rebuff. He paused and wiped an arm across his sweating brow. 'It's like this, Anna, I need the money,' he said in a more propitiatory tone. 'A man cannot go all the way to Glasgow to live without a bit of money at the back of him. It's likely I'll have little enough by the time everything's paid for.'

She said, as she had said to Jeannie, 'Have you not given a thought to what is going to happen to me, Mata?'

'Of course I have. I've been worrying myself sick over it, but, as Jeannie pointed out, it's not as if you're likely to be homeless, is it? There's all our own folk around who would be glad to give you a home in return for work. I was after speaking to Aunt Annie a day or two since and there's no doubt you'd be welcome there. She's finding it a job to get around since she had that fall and hurt her leg.'

Anna rounded on him. 'You mentioned this to Aunt Annie before ever saying a word to me?' He made no denial. Anna's eyes grew cold; her tone was incisive. 'Mata Matheson, you may be my brother and I do not deny you rightfully own this croft, but you do not own me. My life is my own and not for you and your city wife to arrange for me.' Her chin lifted. 'I will certainly not go to live with Aunt Annie. She is mean and crabbit, as well you know, and has driven her own daughter from her with her constant grumbling.' Indignation so clogged Anna's throat that she could not continue.

Mata tried to placate her. 'I'll maybe have a little money to spare from what I'm getting for the croft. Enough to help see you right until you get some place that pleases you,' he offered.

'I will take from you only what is due to me since last rent day,' she declared.

'That's not likely to be much,' he said. 'See, Anna, with the bairn on the way it'll mean putting money aside for that. Jeannie says it costs money to have a bairn in Glasgow.'

'A bairn? You are saying Jeannie is with child?' As her suspicions were confirmed elation gentled Anna's exclamation.

'Aye. She thinks it's pretty certain. That's another reason I agreed to move to Glasgow. Jeannie's dead against the bairn being born here. She says we're too far from a doctor for one thing, and for another she reckons she'll never be able to push the baby around in a pram. Those sort of things mean a lot to Jeannie,' he finished half-heartedly.

'Oh!' Anna's tone was flat. Her soaring hope was dashed mercilessly. There was to be a child but it was likely she would never see it. For an instant she felt almost as if a living child had been snatched from her cradling arms. Yet another layer of coldness superimposed itself on the chill that was already heavy in her stomach. It was a few seconds before she could trust her voice again. 'I will take no money from you other than what is due to me since the last accounting,' she reiterated. 'That much I need and must have and also the money I lent you to go to Glasgow and which you have not yet repaid.' She was aware of her attitude hardening as she spoke. 'The money you will get for selling the croft is yours entirely. I have no wish nor right to take any share of it.' She did not need to tell him that it would make her feel as much a traitor as she now thought him.

Mata's relief was evident. 'That's not the way I wanted it to be but I'll not pretend I'm not glad to hear you say it,' he confessed. 'And I'll not forget it, Anna. If this job in Glasgow turns out to be as well paid as Jeannie thinks it's likely to be, I'll maybe spare a little from time to time, just until you're settled some place.' When she made no comment he tried to lighten the atmosphere between them by adopting a teasing tone. 'How about yourself getting married?' he suggested. 'There's time yet; you're not thirty. And there's time for bairns too if you've a mind.' Insensitive to her feelings and encouraged by her silence, he dared a wink at her. 'There's Black Fergus now,' he went on with an attempt at bravado. 'If he doesn't bring back one of his fancy women from the town to keep house for him he'll be wanting someone to look after him now his mother's dead.' Out of the corner of his eye he saw Anna stiffen and, realizing how repellent she found his innuendo, he tried to compensate by twisting his mouth into an exaggeratedly sardonic grin. His grin faded as he saw the condemnation in her eyes and, throwing down the hayfork, he pushed past her out of the byre.

Watching him go, Anna was assailed by a terrible loneliness. She asked herself whether the gulf between her and Mata had grown too wide ever to be bridged again. As tears filmed her eyes she had to tighten her jaw to prevent herself from sobbing. A sensation of helplessness came over her and she had to hold onto one of the stalls for support. She had never been ill in her life but the interchange with Mata had left her feeling as if she had been weakened by some long and debilitating illness. Not simply weakened but physically bruised, as she recalled having felt when, in her youth, a newly calved cow intent on protecting her calf had caught her off guard and pinned her against the wall of this very byre. Her eyes sought and dwelt on the spot. She had felt trapped and afraid then but her quick wits and young strength had enabled her to free herself before much damage was done. She felt similarly trapped and afraid now though no attacker was visible. But she could summon no resistance. Not only was her body weakened but her mind seemed to have become dull, as if an attack of cramp were robbing her of the power to think how best she could cope with the dilemma which loomed ahead of her.

She slid down onto the piled hay, her hands twisting and pulling at each other as she strove to rise above the despair that gripped her. And at last indignation came to her rescue, a steadily mounting indignation, which brought a hurrying of her heartbeat and a return of strength which helped overcome the dread she felt at having to return to the cottage, helped her to frame the cutting reproaches she intended to level at her brother and her sister-in-law.

Striding purposefully into the kitchen she found it empty and silent. She assumed that Mata had doubtless tried to calm his edginess by going out for an evening's fishing while almost certainly Jeannie would have gone up to intercept the postman to inquire if he had yet brought her the magazines she was so anxiously awaiting. Thus thwarted from her

48

intention, she sat down. The empty kitchen, strange as it still seemed to her with the modern grate and new furniture, nevertheless soothed the turmoil inside her. Anger was for her such an alien emotion that within minutes she was thankful that she had been deflected from her purpose. Since the bitter words that had leaped to her tongue could do no good they were best left unspoken.

She stood up and with dragging feet went to stand in the doorway, looking out across the area of the croft towards the slate-blue sea as she tried to absorb the tranquillity of the evening, breathing in its multiplicity of smells as if striving to anaesthetize herself against her grief. Intuitively she identified them: the salt-spiced air; fresh earth, damp after earlier drizzle; the faraway smell of mingled heather and bracken; the nearby smell of the remains of last year's haystack; the unmistakable smell of poultry; the pervasiveness of peak smoke. From the vicinity of the byre drifted the familiar smell of dried cow dung, while nearer at hand came the more pungent smell of fresh excrement from the milk-fed calves which were still tethered on the croft and which had for some time been reminding her with increasing clamorousness that it was time for their evening feed.

Resolutely she went to the dairy shed and proceeded to fill their feeding pails.

5

As soon as her outside work was finished, Anna, ignoring the meal Jeannie had prepared, resorted to her own cramped bedroom. She had no appetite for food, not even for the fresh fish Mata had caught that evening. The atmosphere would be too strained, she was sure, for them to sit together at the table. Mata would be expecting more looks and words of reproach from her while Jeannie would be only too ready to be combative on his behalf. And Anna wanted no more altercation. Jeannie had stated and now Mata had confirmed that their decision to get rid of the croft was irreversible. There was, as she saw it, nothing to be gained by speaking about the matter further.

Crushed by her brother's perfidy, she lay on her bed staring up at the ceiling and trying to convince herself that before long this room would be occupied by a complete stranger; that the cottage would cease to be her home and that she must seek other accommodation. She turned restlessly, trying to ease the torment that beat at her brain. She did not reach for her Bible as she had been taught to do in times of stress; neither did she pray to the God of whom she was so much in awe. Her parents' acceptance of 'the Lord's Will' had instilled in her a similar fatalism which precluded words of entreaty from reaching her lips. She could only submit, while the wear and tear of dismay and apprehension racked her body and mind. As her bedroom darkened and the night closed in, the hot, unshed tears burned at the back of her eyes while her right hand repeatedly stroked the sleeve that covered her wasted arm.

Jeannie's blunt reference to her arm had shaken her. Anna had never known a time when her one arm had not been less mobile than the other. She herself scarcely noticed it. When in early childhood she had questioned her mother as to the difference, her mother had explained that her left arm had not developed in the same way as her right arm because of an illness during infancy. It was thinner and also twisted so that the hand was turned permanently outwards, but the fingers were very nearly as flexible and the skin was as smooth and freckled as that of her other arm. As soon as she became aware that the arm was defective Anna had been so resolute in overcoming its limitations that she had long ago ceased to regard it as being in any way a liability. Could she not milk a cow and make hay and muck out a byre as well as anyone, she asked herself now. Could she not bake and clean efficiently? Could she not carry peats? Indeed, was there any work connected with the croft at which she could not match herself against any other woman? Had Jeannie not observed this herself? Why then had she implied that her arm was such a disadvantage? No one else had remarked pityingly on it and, though Anna had long since concluded that it may have been one of the reasons that no man had come courting her, Jeannie had been speaking of finding employment, not a husband.

That her sister-in-law had paid little heed to her claim that she had once been considered clever enough to have qualified as a schoolteacher brought home more forcibly the knowledge that it was now too late. Grasping for reassurance, she wished fervently that she had not been forced to neglect her book learning after she had left school. She was

51

now too old to think of becoming a schoolteacher but there could still have been a chance for her to attach herself in some way to the fringes of the profession. But nursing her parents and working on the croft had drained her resolution and now, at nearly twenty-nine years old, she could boast few accomplishments other than being a good worker on the land and a capable housekeeper.

She cast around for ideas. Her friend, the retired schoolmistress who sent her books, had issued an open invitation to her to pay a long visit. Should she risk accepting it now? But if Mata could not pay her the money he owed her how could she pay her fare? No. She had to think of some other alternative. Determined not to impose herself on her kinsmen, it seemed to her that the only prospect of earning her living was to find work where accommodation and food were provided, the other proviso being that it must not be so far away that she would have to spend what little money she had on getting there. She had seen such situations advertised in the weekly paper but guessed that many of them were on farms which were too isolated to attract workers. Others, judging from the frequency with which they appeared, were almost certainly on farms where the conditions were so uncongenial that only halfwits would endure them. The idea came to her that she should insert an advertisment stating her availability. She would have it inserted under a box number and it would have to be done without the knowledge of Jeannie and Mata, which meant that she would have to waylay the postman each day before he came within sight of the house. It would be risky, but if she had the promise of employment to go to she could at least put on a pretence of looking forward to a change in her circumstances. It would save her the trial of having to endure her sister-in-law's offhand commiserations.

She received two replies. One wanting a lady's maid 'who could do fine sewing'. The other, written in a shaky hand, was from a man who needed a companion to lie beside him at night because he was old and because he had such bad dreams he sometimes tried to throw himself out of the window. She looked at her roughened hands. Fine sewing had never been an accomplishment of hers and in any case the address showed it to be too distant for her to afford the journey. Over the old man's letter she managed a smile. 'It's not a companion he's needing but just more water with it,' she mused. With failing hope she waited for other letters to arrive, but the weeks went by and none came.

Except for the half dozen pullets which Anna had insisted were hers to keep until the last moment of her stay, the poultry had been disposed of to neighbours, and now that the cattle and sheep had been sent to the sale the croft looked forsaken. The carrier called to load the furniture and boxes which Jeannie and Mata were taking to their new home and all too soon afterwards came the taxi which was to take them to the mainland ferry. They heard the driver sounding his horn to announce his arrival at the entrance to the croft. Anna walked with them to the road.

'You'll be sure to come and see us once we're settled in, Anna,' Mata invited with careful eagerness. 'She'll surely want to see the new flat, won't she?' he called to Jeannie who was walking a little ahead of them. Jeannie affected not to hear. 'It's going to be grand, right enough, living in a place with taps and electricity and things and plenty going on all round us,' he said with what Anna thought was waning enthusiasm.

'Maybe, someday,' Anna murmured.

Before getting into the taxi Jeannie turned to Anna. 'Well, it's goodbye and the best of luck to you,' she said, holding out her hand.

'And to you,' Anna responded.

Jeannie glanced at her husband. 'And as Mata was saying, if ever you're in Glasgow be sure to drop in and see us.' She was obviously anxious to cool down whatever warmth she had heard in Mata's invitation. She and Anna exchanged stiff smiles.

'Oh, she must come and see the bairn, mustn't she, Jeannie?' Mata urged, plainly wanting the parting to be a cordial one.

'Aye, but see and wear some more up-to-date clothes when you come,' Jeannie chaffed. 'If you arrive in your usual Sunday blacks the neighbours might think you're aiming to put the evil eye or a curse on the bairn.'

Mata laughed uneasily. Anna managed a smile. Jeannie settled herself in the taxi, shouting above the noise of the engine as she joked with the driver. Mata lingered.

'Have you decided yet on your plans?' he asked Anna, and now that Jeannie was out of hearing there was genuine concern in his voice.

'I plan to stay here until the new owners come,' she replied. 'That's not for a while yet, is it?'

'Another three weeks,' he told her. 'That should give you time to look around and make your mind up about what you want to do.' He looked at her anxiously.

'I shall find plenty to do,' Anna assured him. 'There's still a good deal of tidying up to be done around the place before the new folks arrive. Enough to keep me busy until I'm ready to go to my job.'

'You have a job in mind? You didn't tell me, Anna,' he reproached her. 'Where's it to be?'

'Oh, I have the choice of one or two,' she temporized. 'I'll need to think a bit more about which one I shall take.'

She felt her cheeks growing hot under Mata's scrutiny, but he, assuming that her flush was due to vexation at his prying into her affairs in the presence of Jeannie, said in a relieved voice, 'That's grand, Anna. That's really grand.' Grasping each other's shoulders, they exchanged farewell kisses.

'You'll write to me, won't you, Anna? You'll not forget to let me know your new address?'

Pretending her attention had been caught by something in the distance, she deliberately made him wait for her answer, and Jeannie, growing impatient, shouted to him to get into the taxi. He did as he was bidden but, pushing down the window, he leaned out to repeat, 'You will be sure to write now, Anna? I'll want to know where you are and how you've settled.' He seemed at last to have allowed himself to recognize the extent of the injustice he had done to her and now was begging her understanding and forgiveness. His eyes met hers and she saw the shame and pleading there, the same shame and pleading as she had sometimes seen filling his eyes, when, as a little boy, he had sought her help in trying to overcome some obstacle which threatened to defeat him. Again scenes of their shared childhood rushed back into her mind; her resentment against him moderated long enough for her to give him a fond smile.

'I'll write, Mata,' she promised. 'You don't have to worry about me.'

She stood watching the taxi rumbling away along the flinty road and even when it had disappeared from her sight she remained there as if she were, for the time being, incapable of further movement.

The sound of distant voices at last stirred her to activity and she ran swiftly to where a tumbled stone wall of a ruined dwelling would screen her from the view of the women who were now returning from the morning milking of the hill cattle. The women would want only to offer their commiserations but the need to be alone was paramount. In any case, she had no wish to listen to them expressing their condemnations of Mata's conduct, no will to hear them castigating her sister-in-law, no stomach for their sympathy for her own plight. She would have liked at that moment to have become invisible, to slip out of life temporarily so as to have a period of self-communing which, she hoped, would help drain away the bitterness and self-pity and make room for a resurgence of the confidence she had previously had in herself and in her actions. She longed for a renewal of the strength which, from the moment Jeannie had acquainted her with their decision to give up the croft, had rapidly become impaired by sleeplessness and worry.

When the voices had receded far enough into the distance she made her way to the byre intending to occupy herself by giving it a thorough cleaning, but the empty stalls brought back images that were too poignant for her to bear. She went into the barn, but here again, bereft of its complement of hay and corn, it served only to intensify her feeling of hopelessness. Reluctant to return to the cottage, she turned her steps towards the shore and as she descended the steeply winding path she had the sensation that her legs were suddenly less sure of their strength, that her gumbooted feet were less confident when she reached the rough shingle.

She was glad when she got to the cove which until the recent upheaval in her life she had regularly visited to gather driftwood. Now with no purpose other than seeking seclusion she made towards the ivy-screened entrance of a small cave which had once been a favoured haunt for her and Mata. Here in brief spells of childhood ill humour they had sought its concealment to share their indignation; here in periods of adolescent anguish she had come, secretly and alone, to be soothed by watching the complexity of wave patterns and the unceasing rearing and tumbling breakers which hid the deep-down mystery of the sea. Finding a handy seat-sized lump of wood, she carried it to the cave and, squeezing herself in through the narrow entrance, sat down and leaned back against the unyielding rock wall. She found it a comfortable enough position. Until Jeannie had set about transforming the kitchen with new furniture the seating had been only bare wood, straight backed and uncompromising. She had grown up accustomed to its uncushioned rigidity. Pulling aside the overhanging ivy, she stared impassively at the rumpled grey water in which cormorants dived and above which gulls flew in a leisurely way as if reconnoitring the location of their next meal. Tears blurred her vision but they stayed unshed, like crystal droplets in the corners of her eyes. The tide receded, leaving its dishevelled line of wrack and debris; the chill of approaching evening seemed to glaze the water, but still she stayed, content to submit herself to the lenitive effect of the sea until it had dulled the sharper edges of her sadness and its ineffable harmony had mellowed much of her bitterness.

When the light began to fade she rose and was about to leave the cave when the chugging of a boat engine alerted her and, though it was unlikely she could be observed, she shrank back instinctively as a fishing boat rounded the point and steered in a wide sweep towards the cove. She heard the engine being throttled back and as the boat wallowed in the swell she watched the lone figure on board grasp a boathook and begin to haul in a line of lobster creels. There was scorn in her expression as she followed the man's movements. Black Fergus was late enough lifting his creels, she reflected. Very likely one of his fancy women in the town had kept him occupied so he had not noticed the time passing. She experienced a swift feeling of distaste as she recalled her colloquy with Mata in the byre and his throwaway but still stinging allusions as to the eligibility of Black Fergus.

She remained quite still until she had seen him lift and rebait and reset the last creel; until the engine had resumed its urgent throbbing and the boat had disappeared around the point, and then, as a distant lighthouse began to send its beam across the darkening water, she left the cave.

Suddenly realizing she was cold, she set off briskly up the cliff path so as to bring the warmth back to her limbs. She

57

was panting by the time she reached the top and, pausing to regain her breath, she found she was not alone. The figure of a man carrying a sack slung over his shoulder was trudging along a few paces in front of her, obviously having taken a different route up the cliff. Normally her instinct would have been to call out a greeting before joining company with the walker but, recognizing him, she chose to stand still, giving him a chance to get ahead of her.

Black Fergus, sensing there was someone behind him, turned. 'You've surely not been gathering whelks until now?' he addressed her. She was surprised at the affability in his voice.

'Indeed no,' she rejoined, still breathless. 'It is not yet the season for whelk gathering in these parts.'

He slowed his gait as if waiting for her to catch up with him but she made no attempt to do so. The moment became awkward. 'Good fishing?' she inquired, trying to infuse an equal degree of affability into her voice.

'No bad,' he admitted, and moved forward. The path was narrow and, following in his wake, she grew impatient to reach the spot where his path would diverge. Deliberately she lagged farther behind. He stopped and spoke to her over his shoulder. 'I'm hearing your brother's after selling the croft and leaving you with no home to go to.'

Anna made no reply. Everyone knew Mata had disposed of the croft and left her homeless and she had no intention of further commenting on the matter, least of all to a man such as Black Fergus.

'It'll not be so easy finding a job at your age,' he pointed out.

She detected no trace of compassion in his voice. Acidly she retorted, 'The question of whether or not I shall be wanting or needing a job is my own affair, is it not?'

He had begun to move on, but again he stopped, this time to wait until she drew closer. 'So it is, indeed,' he agreed.

There was no mistaking the sneer in his voice and Anna cringed inwardly as his eyes assessed her insolently. They had come now to where their paths diverged and she tried to edge past him, but he stood squarely in her way. 'Seeing my mother's gone, I'm thinking I could do with a woman about the house,' he said. 'Maybe you'll do me.'

Anna's indignation flared. 'And I am thinking there will be no shortage of women of your own kind to choose from,' she flashed back at him.

'You'd do well to think about it,' he advised, letting her outburst glance off him. Turning, he strode on.

'Never!' she cried, and heard in reply his jeering laughter borne to her on the night air.

Sickened and humiliated that he had dared make such an offer, she hurried on, but anger, robbing her of breath, caused her to slow her pace and, struggling for calm, she tried to force the encounter from her mind. Composing herself, she walked on steadily. The village had settled itself into its evening tranquillity. Lamps began to glow in the windows of the scattered cottages; a dim light progressed erratically as someone walked along the road swinging a hurricane lamp. She guessed it would be old Farquar on his way to meet the bus to claim the bottle of whisky he ordered regularly from one of the hotels in the town. A dog barked with sudden hostility. Instantly she identified it as Ruari Bhan's dog and at the same time surmised that Ruari was about to receive a visit from Lahac Euan who had the distinction of being hated by every dog in the village. A man's voice snapped a succession of irritable commands: deaf Peter's recalcitrant cow was evidently giving him more trouble. Katy Beag's unmistakable voice screamed a question to one of her sons and received a gruff reply. She knew it so well, this place where she belonged, that she felt certain she would be able to chart its daily happenings wherever she might be.

Where might she be in three weeks' time? The question

59

troubled her ceaselessly. As she drew nearer to the lamplit windows of the cottages they struck her as being like rescuing hands whose grasp was tantalizingly beyond her reach. She could go into almost any one of them and find a kindly welcome, but had made up her mind not to accept anything more than the traditional hospitality. She made herself consider what it might be like to walk the street of some strange town where, she imagined, the lighted windows would be like peremptory warnings to keep out.

She dawdled homewards, glancing back every now and then towards the sea and the peaks of the mainland hills, which were becoming less emphatic as they merged into the darkness. It felt strange not to be hurrying home at this time of an evening, but now there were no longer cattle to be milked or calves to be fed she was not needed: she was returning to emptiness.

Among the lamplit cottages there were two discernible whose windows as yet showed no glimmer of light. One was the home to which she was now returning, the other, well apart from the rest of the dwellings, was that belonging to Black Fergus. No doubt he preferred to fumble meanly in the dark rather than spend money on paraffin, she assumed.

Inside the cottage she lit the lamp and, turning up the wick, surveyed the familiar room. After Jeannie's new furniture had been loaded onto the furniture van the old table and chairs had been brought back into service for the few days remaining until she and Mata were to take their leave. As a result the room had reverted to the functional austerity Anna had always known. No longer the butt of Jeannie's criticism, the old furniture seemed to be in total repose, as if asseverating its right to be there. The despised coal fire had burned itself into cold ash and cinders. She hurried to rake the grate clean, flinging the ashes outside, not caring where they landed. Bringing kindling and dry peats from the shed, she lit the fire, triumphantly letting it smoke for the first few minutes so the room might regain its characteristic smell. She brewed a pot of tea, boiled a couple of eggs and drawing up the chair which had once been her mother's and had then become hers, she sat by the fire, thinking over the events of the day as she ate her supper.

She had misled Mata about having a choice of jobs to which she could go. She had in fact no prospects and very little money. Less money than she could reasonably have expected at this time of year. Rent day had been back in the spring but then Mata had asked shamefacedly if she would mind waiting a little while longer for her share because he'd had such a pile of bills to pay for all the 'improvements' to the cottage. Unsurprised, Anna had agreed. She had been taught thrift and had saved since earliest childhood, but since she rarely needed money she saw no reason why she should not allow Mata to borrow from her when he needed it. Time went by and when there as still no mention of how much he owed her she bagan to suspect Mata had no money to pay her. Then one day, when he was quite sure Jeannie was well out of the way, he had produced from his pocket a small paper bag.

'Here, take this will you, Anna?' he said, handing it to her in a furtive way. 'There's more to come but I'm kind of short still,' he apologized. 'You understand?'

She had found it easy enough to understand that he was short; not so easy to understand why he was prepared to underpay her and yet, without demur, allow Jeannie to continue overspending. Looking into the bag she had found it contained three pound notes, less than a third of what she was rightfully entitled to, she reckoned. But she would not quarrel with him over money. She could wait for whatever more was due to her. It now looked to her as if she would have to wait a long time. She knew exactly how much money was in the old shortbread tin which she used as her safe and prudently she had decided that what little was there must be saved for possibly a more dire situation than she was now facing. It would be frivolous to spend it on travelling hopefully to some town and then paying for accommodation which might quite conceivably bring no worthwhile result. She had written to several hotels applying for work, but it was the end of the season and they were laying off staff until the summer. It was the end of the busy season for farmwork. The years seemed to stretch before her in an everlasting neverness.

Tiredness suddenly engulfed her and she made ready to go to bed, covering the fire with damp peats, swinging the kettle over to the hob and lighting the candle ready to take through to her bedroom. She moved the lamp from the table to the windowsill but just as she was about to dout it her eye was caught by a piece of cardboard which lay face down on the sill. Picking it up, she saw it was a calendar which had obviously been forgotten or discarded during the rushed last-minute preparations for leaving. It was not the kind of calendar that was usually to be seen in the kitchen of a croft house – not a cheerless one advertising sheep dips and cow balsams and poultry food and also giving gestatory periods for the different animals – but a glossy and gilded one with a separate sheet for each month and each sheet depicting a beautiful woman in different poses against a series of romantic settings. None of the sheets had been torn off and, turning them over, Anna noticed the black pencilled ring which had been drawn around that day's date. She remembered Jeannie drawing Mata's attention to it. 'The twenty-ninth of September. Our red-letter day!' she had gloated. 'The day you and me leave here to begin our new life.' She remembered how Jeannie had held the calendar close to Mata's face, forcing him to look at it; she remembered how, above Jeannie's head, Mata had looked across at her as if pleading for her forbearance.

Anna examined the calendar more closely, curious to see if

62

any other dates had been marked as being of some significance. Jeannie's birthday was ringed as was Mata's, but though it was unmarked one date leaped out at her. The twenty-first of October! Her hand trembled slightly. The twenty-first October was her own birthday. Even as children she and Mata had known no tradition of celebrating birthdays in the family or even in the village and, except for a small coin given to them by their father along with the instruction to put it away safely, and except for their mother's practice of recording the day in a page of her Bible, Anna and Mata's birthdays would have come and gone virtually unheeded. Because she knew her mother would have wanted her to do so Anna had kept up the practice of making the annual entries for herself and Mata, and now, on a sudden impulse, she went through to her bedroom and brought the Bible into the kitchen so as to study it in the stronger light of the lamp. She turned to the hand-written page. It was there plainly enough. On the twenty-first October she would be twenty-nine years old. In just three weeks' time she would be a twenty-nine-year-old woman with no man, no home and no prospect of employment. In three weeks' time the new owners of the cottage would be arriving and before that date she must find some other place to live. The weight of her knowledge made her sag slowly into her chair. I am fit and I am well, but I am already too old to be wanted anywhere, she told herself relentlessly, knowing it to be true. I am too old to try to make for myself a new life among strangers, strangers who, like my sister-in-law, might look at my twisted arm and judge it a disadvantage. I am like an old hen that has had its wings clipped so regularly that it no longer knows the urge to fly. Perhaps it is best that I resign myself to obliterating hope.

Lifting some of the damp peats with which she had smothered the fire, she pushed the calendar down into the still smouldering ash. The calendar itself would be ash by morning. Putting out the lamp, she went through to her bedroom, but the tiredness she had felt earlier was now eluding her and sleep was long in coming. When she woke it was to daylight and to the resolution that she must clear her mind of gloom and force herself to think more positively: to balance her position against her assets; to face up to the conditions she could best endure.

Ten days before her birthday she steeled herself to approach Black Fergus and offer herself as his housekeeper.

6

Black Fergus – the nickname was in no way derogatory but simply referred to his thatch of black hair and his rather swarthy skin – had never been completely accepted by the crofters despite the fact that he had been born in the village. His father, Finlay McFee, had been a true son of the croft, but soon after he had left school Finlay had turned his back on the crofting life and had chosen to go to sea. Except for occasional brief visits home he had remained at sea until his parents had died and he had inherited the croft. By that time Finlay was well on into middle age and, having accumulated a small nest egg sufficient, he considered, to provide a basic income, he had forsaken the sea and returned to his old home, bringing with him a wife, several years younger than himself, whose olive skin and coal-black eyes had marked her as a complete foreigner. During his years of self-imposed exile Finlay had often dreamed of returning to the croft with his wife and had assumed that they would quickly be absorbed into the easy companionship of the village. Alas, from the first moment of her arrival his wife had chosen to isolate herself from all her neighbours, totally rejecting their friendly advances and as a result becoming steadily more reclusive. Scarcely ever did she venture away from the house except after darkness had fallen and then scuttling away quickly if she suspected she was being perceived. 'She's a queer one, right enough,' the crofters had murmured among themselves. 'Ach, give her time,' Finlay would plead ever more hopelessly, until at last he too had come to accept that she was determined never to mix with the villagers.

Ten years after she had come to live in the village Finlay's wife gave birth to a child, the boy Fergus, and her subsequent behaviour had led her neighbours to suspect that the event had affected her brain. Instead of proudly showing off the new baby as normally they would have expected a mother to do, she had become almost deranged in her possessiveness, clutching the child fiercely to her bosom whenever anyone came in sight and allowing her husband only a quick peep beneath the shawls which wrapped it. Instead of welcoming the neighbours when they tried to pay congratulatory visits, she greeted them with such a torrent of screaming and incomprehensible abuse that they had retired, shocked and discomfited, before they got within fifty yards of the door, while the district nurse, intent on carrying out what she deemed to be her duty, was subjected to such a bombardment of peats and other handy missiles that she too had to abandon her attempts to keep an eye on the child's welfare.

Through Fergus's infancy and later childhood, and in spite of Finlay's gentle coaxing, remonstrance and ultimately angry accusations, her possessiveness did not diminish. As if she feared some evil spell might be put upon the child, she would allow no one near him unless Finlay insisted and then only when she could hover over him to protect him from being touched. If anyone dared speak to the boy it was always she who made an answer for him, the result being that by the time Fergus had reached his sixth birthday no one save his parents could say that they had ever heard him utter a single word.

At the evening ceilidhs the behaviour of Finlay's wife was a recurring subject for discussion among the crofters. They theorized on the possible reasons for it and found a smug pleasure in listening to the varying predictions as to what was likely to happen when, in a few months' time, Fergus reached the statutory age for attending school.

Shortly before that time a policeman from the town visited the village asking to be directed to Finlay's cottage. The crofters, watching discreetly, were intrigued to see what the policeman's reaction would be when he was greeted with missiles and abuse. They expected to be awed or amused but were disappointed. Those who were close enough saw that the door of the cottage was opened promptly though by only a few reluctant inches; saw that the policeman appeared to deliver a message; and that immediately he had finished speaking the door slammed shut. Strategically waylaid and offered a 'cup of tea', the policeman disclosed that his message had been a sad one. Finlay McFee had, the previous day, joined with two other men and gone on a fishing trip. No one knew yet what had happened but all three men had been found drowned earlier that morning. Finlay's strange wife had become overnight the Widow McFee. The policeman further reported that before he had been able to attempt to offer his condolences the door closed firmly on him and from the sounds he heard it seemed that it was being barricaded from inside. Even while he had stood listening and debating whether he should persist in trying to offer commiserations and advice there had broken out an uncanny wailing and keening such as he had never heard before and, glad to get away from the place as quickly as he could, he had decided that he could shift any further duty to the widow and her son onto the shoulders of the nurse and the doctor and the minister.

Three days after her husband had been laid to rest in the burial ground the windows of Widow McFee's cottage were seen to have been inexpertly boarded up and a length of rope tied to the door latch and then secured to a bar wedged horizontally across the door frame, a contrivance much used by crofters to secure a cottage during the absence of its owner, not so much against possible intruders but against the assaults of the winter gales. The driver of the cart which had taken the widow and her son early that morning on the first stage of their journey to the mainland reported that he had no idea of their ultimate destination. There had been no farewells and she had given no indication as to how long they intended to be away or whether they had any intention of returning.

The crofters confessed themselves relieved to be rid of the presence of the puzzlingly hostile stranger in their midst, since, despite her antipathy towards them, they realized they could not continue to ignore her as they had resigned themselves to doing when Finlay had been alive. Tradition imposed on them the duty of concern for their neighbours, particularly so if that neighbour were a lone widow with a child. Now the widow's departure absolved them from having to consider among themselves how soon and to what extent they would need once more to sink their pride and risk further rebuffs by attempting to offer help. 'Ach,' they told one another, 'she was a strange one, right enough. Such a one was never meant for a place like this.' So saying, the men had spat and knocked out their pipes and the women had resumed their knitting and all had been content to let the story of the strange woman and her son slip gradually into the folklore of the village.

For thirteen years the widow's cottage stood deserted and uncared for; grass grew on the thatched roofs of the byre and the sheds; their doors slowly rotted on their hinges. The presence of Widow McFee had become hardly more than a legend, and then, to everyone's astonishment, a coal cart from the town arrived one day in the village and, after asking to be directed to the widow's cottage, the driver was seen to be tipping a load of coal beside one of the sheds. The crofters, assuming that the cottage had most likely been sold or let, were naturally overcome with curiosity. It was with scepticism and disquiet they learned that the widow, now nearly crippled with rheumatism, and Fergus, her son, now in his late teens, were soon to be reinstalled there.

There followed a good deal of conjecturing as to the reason for their return, though rumours began to percolate through to the effect that as he had matured Fergus had so strongly rebelled against his mother's possessiveness that he had become what was described as a 'right wild one'. It was said that his suspected involvement in petty crimes had not only earned him the attentions of the police but had made him many enemies, some of whom were reputed to be among the city's most savage thugs. There had come a time when fear of becoming a target for reprisal action by the thugs had kept him so much indoors that his distraught mother, anxiety for her son's wellbeing overcoming her aversion to living on the croft, had prevailed upon him to retreat with her temporarily to the home where he had been born and to remain there until such time as his enemies had wiped him off their blacklist, when his return to his former haunts might be safely contemplated. Whether or not that had been Fergus's true intention was never revealed, but when, after one year had passed and then two years, three and then four and there were no discernible signs that mother and son were making plans to leave the village, the crofters accepted that their residence was likely to be permanent. But though they were in the village the couple were not of it and relations were barely affable. Despite her disabling illness the widow had reverted to her former reclusiveness, repulsing all advances from those who might have helped and befriended her, while Fergus, though not so reclusive, was not considered to be a good neighbour. He neither worked his croft nor would he allow anyone else to work it, which stamped him even more emphatically as an outsider, and the curtly polite greetings which were offered when contact was inescapable were little more cordial than the grunt Fergus gave in exchange.

He then caused some surprise by acquiring a fishing boat, together with creels and other fishing gear, but although to no-one's knowledge had he any experience of boats or fishing, he made no approach to any of the more experienced men to join him in his venture. Had he done so it was unlikely anyone would have agreed, such was his reputation for unpleasantness and cunning, but they were piqued that they had been given no opportunity to refuse. He fished alone, sporadically setting and lifting creels or heading out to sea to set lines and nets. Since he never adhered to the practice of offering a 'fry' of fish to anyone in the village according to custom, they had to rely on other sources for word as to how successful he was being. And report had it that the catches he landed at the mainland port were as good as could be expected from a novice who was fishing alone. Report also had it that what he had left of his takings after visiting the numerous bars was quickly squandered on the many fancy women to whom the fishermen were easy prey, and that it was by no means uncommon for him to end up as a result sleeping off his indulgences in the cuddy of his boat.

Anna was only a few years old and Mata still a baby when the Widow McFee and Fergus had returned so unexpectedly to the cottage. She had never forgotten the stir caused by their reappearance on the scene and during the ensuing years had listened avidly as the resurrected stories of the widow's peculiarities had been recounted. Of Fergus's shady past nothing was said, there being unanimity among the crofters that a man's past was his own business and only for him to divulge should he feel so inclined. They would not perpetuate what might be nothing more than sinful rumour by repeating their suspicions in front of the children. Ignorant of conjecture, Anna and her young friends had formed their own opinion of Black Fergus. To them he seemed aptly named since there was about him an intimidatingly gypsy fierceness which, allied to his scowling expression and gruff voice, made him a figure to be quickly dodged away from when sighted. They had grown used to the idea that he was not a man they would dare pelt, even furtively, with snowballs during winter frolics; not someone on whom they would dare risk playing tricks at Hallowe'en. Among themselves they spoke of him as being 'the queer son of a queerer mother', for in their eyes the scarcely seen Widow McFee had become a sinister image, resembling so closely their idea of a *bandruidh* that they were as careful at keeping their distance from her cottage as they were of keeping their distance from the 'Witch's Bog' out on the moor, where, they believed, if you ventured too close once darkness had fallen, the witch's long, thorny crook would hook onto you and drag you to your doom.

Throughout the years of her adolescence, the years when her hopes of becoming a teacher had been thwarted by having to nurse her parents, and later the years when she and Mata had been working the croft together, Anna had never once gone near the widow's cottage. There had been occasions when she had chided herself for not doing so. The widow was undoubtedly a sick, old woman, and Anna well knew her soft-hearted mother would have urged on her the need to forgive and forget the rebuffs the women of the village had suffered in the past and try once more to extend the hand of friendship. But Anna had not done so. She had set out in that direction one day after having ensured that Fergus was at sea, but, as she had drawn closer, the cottage seemed to be exuding such an air of unfriendliness that her steps had become hesitant and she had changed direction and embarked upon a less awe-inspiring task. She regretted her cowardice when, only a few weeks later and shortly before Mata had shattered her world by telling her he had sold the croft, word had come that the frail old widow had died.

In death as in life the Widow McFee had remained withdrawn. There had been no all-night vigil beside the corpse. Indeed, it was said that Fergus had been callous enough to absent himself and leave the corpse lying alone in the cottage. Since the widow appeared to have no living relatives who wished to attend her funeral there was no whisper of a keening, and on the day of her funeral only those whose company she had shunned felt it their duty to be present to modify the otherwise solitary appearance of her last journey. It was a still day of greyness and gloom when Anna joined the cluster of black-garbed men and women who stood around the coffin where, as was customary, it rested on two kitchen chairs in front of the cottage. Unusually for such an occasion the cottage door was tight closed, so there was shelter neither for the minister nor the mourners from the steady drizzle of rain which was putting a sheen on the plain wood of the coffin and polishing the bare earth where, on a more cared for croft, there would have been some attempt, however slight, to create a garden.

Intrigued as to how the disreputable Fergus was reacting to the death of his mother, Anna scrutinized him covertly while, with bowed head, she listened to the minister intoning the funeral service. Still ignorant of the rumours about his youthful misdemeanours, she wondered why he had chosen to stay in the cottage with his mother when he so obviously preferred the temptations of the town. She wondered if, feeble as she appeared to have been, his mother had nevertheless had some strong hold on her son, whether he had stayed out of devotion or loyalty to her, and whether, now that she was dead, he would desert the croft altogether and return to his former haunts.

She estimated that he must now be around forty-five years old and, according to the conviction of the average crofter, had therefore reached the ideal age when a man should seriously begin to contemplate marriage; an age when he could still be expected to father healthy children who would themselves have reached the right age – that is, too young to marry and yet old enough to support him – when he himself was too old to work. Assessing him as he stood stolid and unemotional behind the byre, Anna thought he looked older than his years. She put the reason down to his debauchery. His hair was still thick and black, as were his shaggy eyebrows, and the black eyes he had inherited from his mother were still lit with the arrogant gypsy fierceness which, as children, she and her friends had found so intimidating; but the mist of hair on his unshaven face was grey and beneath it the scowl lines revealed themselves as being deeply etched. It occurred to Anna that it must be the remnants of gypsy fierceness that was the main attraction for the kind of women he consorted with. In stature he was of much the same height as the rest of the men present, around the six-foot mark, but whereas they were sturdy and straight-shouldered his shoulders were hunched and his body was more rounded, giving him the appearance of being shorter.

She had noticed him shifting from one foot to the other during the ceremony; noticed too that the moment the minister closed his prayer book Fergus was so precipitate in seizing the inkle tape with which the chief mourner asserted his right to lead the coffin to the burial ground that the men who were to take turns at carrying the coffin barely had time to position themselves in readiness before he was striding forward as if impatient to have the whole ceremony concluded.

He made no attempt to observe the unwritten code of solemnly shaking hands with each of the women mourners who had felt it obligatory to attend the funeral and who were waiting in the rain to see the cortége start on its way. He did not make even the most perfunctory acknowledgement of their presence. The women, though not eager to have their hands shaken by such a man, were nevertheless offended that they had been ignored and murmured among themselves as they dispersed. Much of the murmuring was condemnatory; some expressed the hope that since he was a disgrace to the village he would now depart. Anna found herself in complete agreement.

Mata, returning from the burial ground, announced that not one single dram of whisky had Fergus offered the men in return for their attendance – a heinous offence never before committed at any funeral within memory – and that as soon as the grave had been sufficiently filled in Fergus had, without a word to anyone, rushed off in the direction of the creek where he kept his boat. The last glimpse anyone had of him was at the helm of his boat, steering well out to sea. For more than a week there was no light in the window of his cottage, but then he came back and resumed his fitful occupation though it was noticed that his absences became lengthier.

7

Not wishing to be observed, Anna waited until after darkness had fallen before she set out to visit Fergus, and at every step she took she had to whip up her failing resolution. She knocked twice on the door and once on the window before any sound of a response reached her. Her heart thumped violently as the door opened and, as if intent on blocking her entrance, Fergus stood slouched against the doorpost, a spent match gripped between his teeth. He looked her over for several seconds after she had stated her purpose in coming.

'There'll need to be a wedding,' he declared.

Her head jerked up in amazement and, horrified that he seemed to have misunderstood her offer, she grew hot with shame and dismay. 'No! No!' she was quick to deny. 'There will certainly be no wedding. I have thought over what you said the other evening and I am now telling you I am prepared to keep your house and also to work the croft for you if that is what you wish. Just that and no more.' Her mouth primmed as pride reasserted itself. 'I would not for one moment consider marrying you,' she stressed.

With a shrug he half turned as if he was about to go back into the house. 'Please yourself,' he said. He let the spent match rest on his lower lip. 'I say there'll have to be a wedding between the two of us or you can take yourself back where you belong.' He shot her a sly glance. 'That's if you belong anywhere now,' he added.

Smarting at his effrontery, she was tempted to leave instantly but, if only to save her own dignity, she felt she must insist in clarifying the exact terms of her offer. 'Am I not making it clear to you that there will be no obligation on your part? Am I not telling you that I will work without reward and, what is more, if I do not suit you and you wish me to go I give you my solemn promise I will do so.' She paused, waiting for some intimation that he was considering what she was saying. 'If you fear I shall be wanting a wage from you, believe me, that is not so. If you will agree to my keeping the few hens I have in one of the sheds which you do not use I would ask for nothing more from you than what I would be needing for housekeeping.' She spoke slowly and deliberately, determined that he should have no illusions regarding her offer. He appeared to be paying little heed to her. 'Am I not offering you a good bargain?' she challenged desperately.

'Marriage!' he reiterated flatly. He moved again but only to adjust his slouch.

She stared at him, shaking her head in an obtuseness of understanding. 'But why?' she breathed. 'What reason have you for making such a condition?'

'Why? Why?' he mocked. 'Well, don't be thinking I'll be after wanting your body. You'll be only too welcome to keep that to yourself. I've plenty of younger women than you eager to pleasure me.' He was watching her closely as he spoke, as if hoping to see her wince at his rejection of her, but her gaze stayed on him unwaveringly, silently countering his boorishness. 'Why indeed?' he continued. 'Then I'm telling you why since you'd best know the reason for it. There has to be a wedding because once it got known in the town that I was living regularly with a woman I'd not been wedded to some of the most important folk would be for turning against me.' His reasoning struck Anna as being so naive that it was on the tip of her tongue to taunt him with his already infamous reputation. Before she could speak he continued, 'There's some of them there that are so bloody God-fearing they're as like as not to turn their noses up at buying fish from me because of it. I'm not taking any risk of that happening, so that's the reason I say there's got to be a wedding,' he explained. 'I wouldn't be bothering myself otherwise.' He flicked her over with a glance of total disinterest.

Swamped by a feeling of complete incredulity, Anna could only gape at him. She wanted to laugh but knew she dare not. She wanted to close her eyes tightly to shut out the sight of him but knew she must not in case he should interpret it as a sign of weakness. She wanted to turn and walk away with such immense dignity that he could not fail to be aware of the contempt she felt for him but was conscious of a sudden lack of strength in her legs which she feared might cause her to stumble and thus make her look ridiculous. She felt as if she was having to dredge the breath up from her stomach so as to brace herself to return his rudeness.

'Do not the folks in the town buy your fish when surely it must be better known there than anywhere else that you make a habit of drunkenness and whoring.'

Something that might have been a smile sped across his face. 'Surely,' he agreed, picking the match off his lip and flipping it into the darkness. 'But they have to turn a blind eye to that seeing there's others just as guilty among themselves.' His mouth twisted scornfully. 'But living regular with one woman in my own home without being married to her, that would be different.' He shook his head with spurious gravity. 'That now would be a sin in their eyes and they'd have to find some way of letting the minister know they didn't hold with it. It would no doubt be the minister himself who would set them against me and tell them to stop buying my fish.'

77

'Then I suggest you marry one of your street women,' Anna advised, her eyes brilliant with contempt.

He gave a grunt of coarse laughter. 'Marry one of them? I'd be as well marrying a cat,' he told her. 'There's not one of them good for anything but what they do. No, I've a mind now to keep a cow or two and maybe grow some potatoes. Make more use of the croft, you understand? And I'd need a proper woman for that.'

'A proper woman?' Anna echoed.

'Aye,' he said, missing the irony in her voice.

Still waiting until she had regained enough composure to be sure of making a dignified retreat, she observed, 'You never attempted to work your croft when your mother was alive. Why should you wish to do so now she has passed on?'

'A man cannot have one foot on a boat and the other on the land at the same time without help,' he defended. 'And my mother could never have looked after any part of the croft. Or would not,' he corrected. 'She had no liking for the beasts of the fields and little enough for the fruits of the earth. She wasn't one for these parts at all. But you,' he treated her to a shrewdly calculating stare as if he might have been assessing the merits of an animal in the sale ring, 'I reckon you'd do fine for what I'm wanting.'

Disgust regenerated Anna's strength. She glared at him. 'What you are wanting you will not get from me, Fergus McFee,' she snapped, and, treating him to a sardonic bow, she stalked away, her back stiff with hauteur.

'Mind now,' she heard him call after her, 'I'll promise I'll not be asking to share your bed.'

Anger had hurried her back to the cottage; an uncharacteristic anger that had blunted despair and goaded her to frenzied activity. Despite the hour and despite having already cleaned out the peat shed, she now lit the hurricane lamp and tackled the shed anew, restacking the peats which remained and sweeping the dry earth floor until scarcely a fibre of peat dross could be seen on it. And while she worked the exchange with Black Fergus raged through her mind. Marry him! Never! The thought filled her with sick detestation. Nothing would induce her to do so. She railed against his treatment of her at the same time as she punished herself for what she now thought of as her own lack of modesty in daring to approach him.

The decision to offer herself as his housekeeper had been a mortifying one, arrived at only after prolonged despair had left her feeling so vulnerable and unwanted that at the time it seemed to her to be the only course left open. The thought of sharing a house with a man who was well known to be boorish and immoral was utterly repugnant, but, reminding herself that he spent so much of his time either on his boat or indulging himself in the pleasures of the town, she had judged that the task of acting purely as his housekeeper might prove less unpleasant than having to take whatever job was offered in a place where she would be a stranger. At least by staying here she would be in familiar surroundings; she would still have the freedom of the moors, the solace of the sea and the glory of the hills to counteract the tendency to repine. She could make his home clean and neat as he might wish it to be and, save as it affected the provision of his meals, it would be none of her business to concern herself with his comings and goings. Still less would it be up to her to criticize his behaviour. They might share the same roof but their lives would be entirely separate. Such an arrangement seemed to Anna to be workable and acceptable.

Knowing his reputation for meanness, she had imagined that, with the proviso that she would be willing to do most of the work entailed, he would be amenable to her keeping some livestock on the croft, thus obviating the need to spend money on milk and eggs. She had forseen that, with animals to tend, plenty of croft work to keep her occupied and a room of her own to resort to when work was done, she and Fergus could be virtually invisible to each other. For her part, she would have a foothold in a home that, even without concord, could make a tolerable lodging.

Had it ever occurred to Anna that Fergus would mention the word 'marriage', she would have instantly expunged him from her consideration of possible solutions to her problem. Her conviction had been that he would be only too pleased to have found someone who would work for him not only without wages but without requiring him to commit himself in any way. The word 'marriage' coming from him had so astounded her that it had left her chokingly incapable of telling him bluntly how much she despised him. The words flew to her throat now and, as she banged shut the door of the peat shed and looked across to where the light from his window glowed feebly, she had to stifle an impulse to go there and acquaint him of her opinion of him. The sight and sound of him flashed across her mind. 'Not for your body!' His utterance had seemed an outrage. She leaned wearily against the door. 'I'll not be wanting to share your bed.' She had little doubt that his parting remark had been intended to reassure and perhaps to encourage her to accept his proposal but the ugly words still chafed, adding obscurely to the sense of impairment which had been first induced by Jeannie's insensitive reflection on her deformity.

In her bedroom Anna flung herself face downwards on her bed, pressing her hands against her hot, shamed cheeks as she tried to obliterate the scene from her mind. She would have to leave the village now, she warned herself, for surely Black Fergus would live up to his reputation and would soon be giving a gloating and distorted account of the reason she had visited him. She would have to use what little money she had to enable her to get away. As she saw it there was no alternative.

The following morning she was returning from the well when she saw Fergus emerge from behind a corner of the barn

80

looking as if he was intent on waylaying her. Too broken now for anger and with her pride almost in tatters, she stood, looking beyond him, her face closed tight against any approach she suspected he was about to make.

He said nonchalantly, 'I'm hearing there's to be a cattle sale on Tuesday in Struan. I'm thinking maybe I'll bring back a heifer or two to have on the croft and maybe a few sheep.' His voice was in no way interrogative and Anna expressed no interest. 'I reckon there's time yet to make a fair bit of hay supposing I start scything today.' He glanced at her pointedly. 'D'you think I should do that?'

A tiny thread of forbearance worked its way into Anna's hostility. 'Maybe you'll be lucky with the weather,' she allowed, speculating on the significance of the huddle of white cloud which appeared to be resting, motionless, on the horizon. With a swing of her shoulders she made a move to pass him.

'Seeing you've not much to do around your place, I'm thinking maybe you'd keep an eye on the hay for me while I'm on the sea.' He inclined his head in the direction of his croft. 'And maybe see to the cattle when they come.' As if it was an afterthought he added, 'You could live in the house, the same as I said last night.'

Anna put down the two pails she was carrying. She knew that because she was only a woman and because they both belonged to a male-dominated society his oblique questioning was the nearest he would ever be able to get to making an appeal. She considered her reply, recognizing that the yearning to stay and to have again the welfare of animals in her care was threatening to overcome the loathing she still felt for being linked with him even nominally in marriage.

Folding her arms across her chest she faced him. 'You said last night that were I to agree to marry, you would not want my body?'

'I said that,' he affirmed.

81

'Will you now swear that you will never claim the right to do so?' she demanded. Half expecting him to make some unflattering reply, she was ready with the suitable riposte.

'I'll swear to it,' he vowed. 'It's the truth I'm telling you. You can keep your virtue so far as I'm concerned. There,' he went on sulkily, 'is there anything else you're wanting to bind me to?'

'You must promise to provide me with money for housekeeping whenever I need it. I shall be frugal with it as I have always been with my own.'

'Aye, surely you'll get that,' he snapped.

In Anna's view the union, such as it was to be, was sealed then. She picked up her pails. 'I'm thinking the weather will hold,' she told him. 'You would be safe enough to start scything the grass.'

A week later they were legally married.

8

The ceremony, which she had wished to be as discreet as possible, and which, because she was not prepared to allow her old home to be the setting for such spurious vows as would be made, took place in the home of Aunt Annie, was almost dismissive in its brevity. The atmosphere was strained; the minister taciturn; her cousin Alistair, who was the only other witness, betrayed his disapproval of the union by making no attempt at the usual joviality normally associated with such occasions. Once the meagre toast had been drunk and the almost as meagre good wishes had been expressed, the minister and Alistair made little attempt to mask their eagerness to depart, and as soon as they had gone Fergus made a gruff acknowledgement to Aunt Annie and went to the door.

'Ready?' His voice was brusque.

Anna nodded. Picking up the suitcase she had packed in readiness that morning and taking the can of milk Aunt Annie proffered she followed Fergus until they reached his cottage, where he swiftly donned oilskins and thigh boots, and, muttering that it was high time he went to attend to his creels, pushed roughly past her and went out through the door. To her immense relief she realized that she had been left alone to introduce herself to her new home.

Standing in the kitchen, she surveyed it with tight-lipped determination. There was no welcome in it. No attempt had been made to clean or disguise the neglect it had suffered since his mother's demise. The fire grate was choked with long-dead ashes; the dust-covered hobs showed patches of rust. The linoleum-covered floor was barely visible beneath the mud of unwiped boots, and she guessed that the hearthrug, which was caked with dirt, was very likely the cause of the stale smell of the room. She tried to open the window but found it jammed fast and with a sigh of exasperation went out into the pale sunlight, leaving the door wide open to the fresh air while she investigated the outbuildings.

The first shed contained finished lobster creels and the materials for making and repairing them, while adjoining it was a small shed which housed a mound of coal. A few yards distant was a stone-built thatched shed which had obviously once been a dwelling house but which had then been replaced by the cottage presently in use. Yet another shed, built from driftwood and roofed with felt, gave evidence of having once been used to house poultry. She contemplated the buildings with satisfaction. She could soon repair the perches and nestboxes in the poultry shed, making it ready for the pullets she had insisted on keeping; except for cutting rushes to repair the dilapidated roof of the old house, there would not be a great deal of work necessary to make it suitable for use as part byre and part barn.

Returning to the cottage, she again surveyed the kitchen. There were signs that it had once been cared for as well if not better than many croft kitchens and, freed from its grime, it could soon be given a homely appearance. Her gaze rested on the dingy curtains which covered the recess bed where, she surmised, Fergus slept when he was at home. Tentatively she drew back the curtain. An expression of distaste crossed her face as she saw the dishevelled and heavily soiled bedclothes, the ticking pillow with its greasily brown indentation where his head had rested, the discarded woollen socks and dirt-streaked underwear that were strewn haphazardly on and under the bed. She drew the curtain to screen it. It was going to be part of her duty to see that everything was kept in a less squalid state in future but for the moment she rebelled at the idea of touching it, telling herself that since Fergus had been used to sleeping in such conditions for some time he could continue to do so until she had cleaned the rest of the kitchen to her satisfaction.

Taking her suitcase, she crossed the porch and stood apprehensively outside the door of the only other room in the house as if she was about to enter forbidden territory. This must have been his mother's bedroom, and as she lifted the latch Anna tried to shake off the lingering tendrils of childhood superstition. The door swung open creakily and to her surprise revealed a room that was rather more cheerful and attractive than had been her own bedroom at home. An empty bedstead, bare of mattress and coverings, occupied much of the space, but against one wall was a marble-topped washstand complete with flower-decorated ewer and basin such as she had seen in the bedrooms of the laird's house when one of her relatives, who had been a servant there, had taken her on a sly tour of inspection. Behind the door was a large chest of drawers, on top of which lay two tapestry cushions looking as if they might be waiting for a suitable chair on which to repose. The floor was covered by a rose-patterned linoleum and a well-brushed sheepskin lay beside the bed. Contrasted with the functional furnishings of her own home, the room struck her as having an air of opulence about it and, much heartened, Anna ventured farther, continuing to look about her with lively interest. The old woman, witch as she was reputed to have been, had left no detectable aura of sorcery behind her. Rather, she appeared to have been as normal as most women so far as an appreciation of what could be called luxury had been concerned.

Banishing the last remnants of superstition, Anna turned her attention to the latch of the door. As she had suspected, there was no way of securing it against would-be intruders and, despite Fergus's solemn vow, she determined to find a piece of wood which she could wedge between the latch and the bracket of the latch so as to prevent it being lifted, a trick she had often used on the similar latch of her own bedroom to deter young Mata from bursting in upon her.

Opening her suitcase, she changed from the blouse and skirt she had worn for the wedding into her working clothes and then returned to the kitchen. She contemplated first the empty grate. Despite Jeannie's liking for coal fires Anna abhorred them, but since the need for plenty of hot water was urgent and there were no peats available for her to use she had to wrestle with the intricacies of setting such a fire and coaxing it to burn. Irritated by the number of attempts she had to make, she resolved that, rather than leave the peats which remained in the shed at the old home for the use of the new owners, it would be advisable for her to have them brought over for her own use. It would not be difficult. Her cousin Alistair had promised to come over later that day with his horse and cart and bring her own mattress and bed linen and the few possessions she wished not to be parted from such as her books and her clothes chest, her mother's chair and the iron girdle and oatcake toaster, which Anna regarded as being indispensable. Alistair would then be making a second journey to bring her pullets and what was left of their corn so there would be ample space on the cart for the remaining stock of peats.

Once the fire had heated innumerable kettles and pans of water and she was satisfied she had made the room as clean and fresh as she could with the few implements she had been able to locate, she brewed a pot of tea and sat down to review what she judged were the more pressing tasks she must perform before she could consider the cottage habitable.

Hovering at the back of her mind constantly was the dread that Fergus might return before she had had time to achieve what she proposed to do, which was to have her own meal while he was absent and then to have his meal ready for his return. While he was eating she could busy herself with whatever work the light permitted her to do and then she reckoned she would need only to wash the dishes and put them away before escaping to her own room, where, remembering to wedge the latch, she could become absorbed in a book and hope to disregard the unsettling knowledge that he was only a few strides away from her across the porch.

With a sudden thrust of something like panic the problem of what food she must prepare for his evening meal reared itself and, hastily putting down her cup, she went through to the pantry. Her nose wrinkled with disgust as she opened the door and was met by the compounded smells of mould and mice, rancid fat and stale fish. Gingerly lifting the lid of what looked to be the flour girnel, she discovered its contents to be heaving with weevils, and as soon as she saw the carelessly replaced lid of the oatmeal chest she guessed, correctly, that she would find the meal liberally threaded with mice droppings. A pail half full of mouse-nibbled potatoes stood on the floor beneath the shelf, while in a dark cobwebby corner stood a covered crock which proclaimed malodorously that it still contained the relics of the previous season's supply of salt herring. Closing the door, she turned her attention to the cupboards of the kitchen dresser. Surely the man must eat when he's at home, she reasoned, but only a limp cardboard box containing a collection of half-used packets of indigestion remedies and stomach powders gave evidence that he must do so. She had to assume that he brought food with him each time he came home, but sooner than rely on her assumption she decided it was better not to risk giving Fergus even the flimsiest grounds for complaint against her. As a gesture of welcome she had left a small supply of flour and oatmeal and salt fish in the pantry at her former home in case the new owners should arrive without having taken the precaution of bringing food with them. Now she knew she could not afford the gesture. The food was needed here and, in addition to the eggs she could expect to collect from the pullets, she calculated it would be sufficient to provide for both her and Fergus until the arrival of the weekly grocery van.

She was searching for a sack in which she could carry back the food when she was hailed by a shout from outside. To her relief Alistair was waiting there with his horse and loaded cart. 'My, am I glad to see you, Alistair!' she greeted him and felt instantly rebuffed when his reply was not equally cordial. Almost as instantly she knew she should not have expected it to be so. Alistair had not concealed his disapproval of her plan to marry Black Fergus and had agreed to witness her wedding only because his gentle nature made it difficult for him to refuse any favour asked of him. She had not had to ask him to let her have the use of his horse and cart to help her move her few possessions to her new home. He had volunteered to do so, but she knew she should not have expected him to show any enthusiasm for the task. As they worked together unloading and carrying in the contents of the cart, uneasiness lay between them like a spiky hedge, and instead of conversing naturally they jerked only monosyllabic remarks and instructions at each other.

When unloading had been completed, she offered him the obligatory cup of tea; he refused it, saying that Lexy, his wife, was waiting on him to help her dose a sick calf. They were both aware that it was a feeble pretext but Anna, loth to embarrass him, tried no persuasion. His promise to come next morning was curt and, as she stood by the door watching him turn and lead away the horse, she had a heightened awareness of how deeply her marriage to Fergus had bewildered and upset her kinsfolk. Their condemnation would be palpable though unspoken and she had been confident that she had conditioned herself to withstand it, but this first evidence of it as displayed by even the soft-hearted Alistair brought a sharp reminder of her continuing vulnerability. She told herself that the estrangement between her and her kinsfolk would not last long. Their innate tolerance would bring them eventually to an understanding of her decision to do as she had done and once she had settled in her new home and could offer them a kind of welcome to the cottage which hitherto had been so forbidding she felt certain that curiosity would draw a warmer response from them. There might even come a time when they had cause to review their opinion of the new Fergus who, in moments of supreme optimism, she naively dared to hope might gradually emerge once he had become accustomed to having a well-run home and croft. She pulled herself up short, realizing that her hopes were threatening to outdistance her reasoning. She must deny herself the harbouring of such fantasies.

There was not time for further contemplation, gloomy or encouraging. It was imperative that she should get hold of some food. The prospect of having to enter the home to which she had said an anguished goodbye earlier that morning made her feel wretched but she knew it had to be faced. The evening was slowly darkening and, the thought occurring that Fergus might return before she could get back, she thought it wise to light the lamp and thus reassure him she was still in the vicinity of the cottage. With the food in a sack slung over her back she was plodding back to Fergus's cottage when a faint tweak of satisfaction pierced her despondency and caused her to pause. The window of the cottage was glowing in the distance more brightly than she had noticed it before, blazoning, it seemed to her, the evidence of her labour in cleaning the smoked-up chimney of the lamp and also the coating of grime and salt which had obscured the windows. She hoped others would notice it and regard it as a portent of change. Her moment of satisfaction was succeeded by a return of disquiet. What if Fergus had returned and was there inside the cottage waiting for her? How would he acknowledge her? How should she acknowledge him? Which of them would be the first to speak?

As soon as she opened the door she saw he was not there and neither was there any sign that he had returned during her absence. Anxious to give him no cause for possible fault-finding, she immediately set about preparing a meal in readiness for him when he did arrive, but so as to avoid having to sit down at the table with him she ate her own share of the meal the moment it was ready. The rest she set to keep hot on the hob and while she waited for the sound of his approach tried to conquer her jumpy nerves by taking up her knitting. It was after midnight when she gave up waiting and went through to her bedroom where, after wedging the latch, she lay on the bed without undressing and without douting her candle for fear she should need to rise quickly and attend to Fergus. The candle burned low and she pinched out its flame, but still she listened with a compulsion that held back sleep for the first sign of his coming. There was an indication of dawn in the sky before she slept at last and when she woke in full daylight Fergus still had not come.

True to his promise Alistair arrived early bringing her crated chickens, a sack of corn and the rest of her peats along with a pail of fresh milk which Lexy had insisted he should bring. Anna welcomed the gift of milk, not simply because without milk her tea would be unpalatable but because she saw it as a consolatory offering intended to demonstrate that though she had upset them she was not to be entirely excluded. But again when she offered him tea Alistair professed to be in a hurry; again she knew it was an excuse, but though his refusal still disappointed her she would not allow herself to worry over it. Acceptance of her marriage would come eventually. She had only to be patient.

She spent the morning in the old henhouse hastily repairing the nestboxes and perches with nails and a hammer she had found in Fergus's creel shed, and when that was done she carried the crate of chickens into the shed and set them free. Next she set about the byre, trying to make it ready for any cattle Fergus might buy. Again towards evening she cooked a meal; again she ate alone and left the rest to keep warm beside the fire; again it was after midnight before she went to her room; and again she rose to another day to find the meal untouched. She began to wonder, half in hope, half in disbelief, whether Fergus's scheme had been simply to get her to look after his home and croft while he made his home elsewhere.

The following day a stranger arrived and announced that he had brought one milking cow and two in-calf heifers which, he said, Fergus had bought at the sale and had instructed him to deliver. The man gave no news of Fergus save that he had been at the cattle sale, and though Anna would have liked some indication of her husband's whereabouts and intentions she was too proud to make any attempt, even obliquely, to elicit any information from the stranger. After the man had departed she enticed the cow into the byre and, feeling its udder, knew that a milk supply was ensured for the future. The two heifers she drove out onto the croft to graze the aftermath and it was as she was returning that she saw Fergus entering the cottage. Her spirits quailed at the sight of him and she had to force herself to follow him inside. He stood beside the table holding a string of fresh-caught mackerel. She darted a quick glance at him, saw that he was not looking at her and glanced away again. Fergus slung the fish carelessly on the table.

'I'm wanting these cooked with my potatoes.' The gruff instruction was his only acknowledgement of her presence.

91

She gave the faintest of nods in reply. He slouched into his chair, flinging his cap with the skill of long habit in the direction of the recess bed. He glared at the newly washed curtain which screened the bed but made no comment. The smell of drink on him was fouling the kitchen; the air seemed to have become suddenly brittle with his smouldering ill humour. Anna, wondering if his was going to explode, built up the fire with dry peats so he should have no cause to complain of being kept waiting for his food.

She had not gone the length of preparing a meal for him but the potatoes were already scrubbed and in the pot and the kettle was full of boiling water to cover them. Deftly Anna filleted the fish before dipping them into oatmeal and pressing them into the pan and while she worked her mind was as busy as her fingers. Since she had used up all the supply of food she had brought from her home she now needed money to buy more. It was necessary for her to tackle Fergus about the housekeeping allowance he had promised to provide and she was debating whether it might be better to wait until he was sober before she asked him or whether he might be more tractable while he was drunk? After she had set the food before him, instead of finding an excuse to go outside, she busied herself about the kitchen while watching him covertly. When his plate was half cleared she decided to risk speaking to him.

'Fergus, there is between us the matter of money for housekeeping,' she charged him. He flicked her a cagy glance and went on eating. 'I must have some money to buy food,' she insisted.

'There's plenty food out the back there,' he nodded towards the larder. 'That is unless you've managed to guzzle your way through it in the few days you've been here.' He snickered, blowing pieces of half-eaten potato back onto his plate. 'And the mackerel I've brought will last a day or two. There's no cause for you to be whining at me for money yet.'

Anna put her hands on the table and leaned forward. 'The potatoes you are eating are some which were left behind in my own home and that is the last of them,' she told him. 'As for there being plenty of food here, I may tell you that the flour that was in the bin was so stale it was crawling with weevil; the oatmeal was riddled with mice droppings and not fit to be eaten. The same can be said for the salt herring and the potatoes.'

'I've been eating it,' he said, glaring at her as he wiped the hairy back of his hand over his grease-filmed lips. 'You can do the same or you can go without. Or maybe buy some with your own precious money if you're so particular,' he added.

'Neither you nor I can eat it,' Anna retorted, a tinge of triumph in her voice, and when he shot her an aggressive look she explained, 'I made the whole lot of it into a mash and fed it to the hens I now have here.'

'Bloody waste!' he broke in truculently.

'No,' she opposed him, 'not wasted. The eggs you are eating along with your fish were laid by those same hens. And if you have a mind to them there will likely be more for your breakfast.' She waited for his comments but when he made no effort to reply she went on, 'And as for buying food with what little money I have of my own, not only was it no part of our bargain but it would buy scarcely enough to feed two folks for a week.' To her chagrin he continued to ignore her. 'Did you not pledge yourself to give me a regular sum for housekeeping?' she pursued. 'If you intend going back on your promise I can in turn go back on mine. While you have been away, the Dear only knows where, I have been spending my time working in your interests but unless you are prepared to allow me money for housekeeping I shall no longer do so.' She felt jittery inside but her voice was firm and as she refilled his mug of tea her eyes were on his, daring him to refuse.

With a muttered epithet he reached into a pocket and threw a note on the table. 'That's what I gave my mother;

that's what I said you'd get and it's plenty. And don't you be wasting a penny of it,' he snarled.

Anna was pleased enough with the amount. She felt certain she could housekeep on less than Fergus's mother had needed. Without hurry she folded the note and put it into the pocket of her apron. 'Of the two of us under this roof, I would say only one of us had the opportunity to waste money,' she told him pointedly.

Banging his knife and fork on the table, he twisted round in his chair to face her. 'You'd best start learning to hold your tongue, woman!' he warned. She raised her eyebrows, challenging him as he glowered at her intimidatingly.

She went to take his empty plate. 'Give me some more!' he commanded, pushing the plate towards her.

She left him still eating his meal; and went out to the byre, telling herself that she was doing so only to check that the cow was content in her stall with plenty of hay and water, though she knew the real reason was simply that she wanted to get away from him. When she returned she found him slumped over the table, his head resting on his folded arms, and since he made no sign of having heard her come in she assumed him to be asleep. Stealthily, so as not to disturb him, she cleared away the remains of the food and washed the dishes and when that was done she lit her lamp ready to take to her own room. She stood for a moment looking at the kitchen lamp, uncertain as to whether she should turn down the wick so as not to risk an accusation of wasting paraffin or whether it might be wise to wake Fergus sufficiently to convey to him that he would sleep more comfortably in his bed. As if her thoughts had penetrated his sleep he stirred, grunting as he changed position. With quick resolution she said, 'Fergus, do you wish me to turn down the lamp before I go to my room?' His head lifted and though his eyes opened they were glazed with sleep. He blinked stupidly and she

94

guessed he was having to struggle to comprehend what she had said.

'Go to hell, woman!' he growled as he let his head slump back on his arms.

She went quickly out of the kitchen and in her bedroom not only wedged the latch but also dragged her clothes chest to block the door. Reason told her she had no need to be afraid; that Fergus was far too drunk to be conscious of her presence in the house; that in his present condition he would be incapable of forcing himself upon her even had he the desire to do so. She undressed and got into bed; her eyelids were heavy; her body felt ready to fall to pieces with tiredness after the events and exertions of the day but she could not relax. Her mind stayed locked on her fear; her nerves stayed too tremblingly aware of Fergus's menacing presence only a couple of strides away across the passage.

9

During the two years that followed her marriage to Fergus Anna had adjusted herself to a pattern of living which, though more solitary than she had previously known or had expected to experience, was in many ways no more insupportable than she had envisaged having to endure. It suited her that Fergus appeared to shrug off any idea of adjusting himself to marriage. The fact that he now had a wife made no noticeable difference to his way of life. He continued his erratic comings and goings, giving no reasons and making no explanations, using the cottage simply as a place where he could demand to be fed and looked after while he recuperated from the spells of dissipation in which he was reported to indulge during his absences in the town.

Anna welcomed his absences, dreaded his homecomings; but since he had continued to show not the slightest interest in her as a woman she had gradually suppressed the fear he might attempt to molest her. Passively she had come to accept her role as a kind of licensed drudge, the inexpectation of kindness from him insulating her against his churlishness much as the inexpectation of ever being warm insulates one from the bitter cold. The coarseness of his language no longer caused her to wince; a bruised and blackened eye had taught her to remain mute when his drunken lumberings threatened disaster in the kitchen. Her earlier hopes that time and a comfortable home might have some softening effect on him had ceased to sustain her. Nothing she did pleased him so she no longer tried to do so. He was, she realized, and would always be a brutish, uncouth fellow – not violently, so that she feared for her life, but rough and abusive whenever there was an opportunity. Deadening her mind to him, she became skilful in avoiding him when he was at home, but even when it was impossible to do so, such as when she was preparing a meal and he came into the kitchen, they continued to repudiate each other, seldom communicating save by crisp, flat-voiced question and answer.

The savage winter storms which kept Fergus's boat tied up in the more sheltered harbour of the port resulted in his spending less time at home and in giving Anna.more time for the periods of repose which helped buttress her spirits to cope with his return. While the gales raged around the cottage she would sit alone by the fireside absorbed in reading and knitting without the constant dread of the door being flung open to herald the entrance of her husband. She made time to visit neighbours, hoping that by so doing she might soon put an end to the estrangement between herself and them, but their welcome was polite rather than warm and when she pressed them to return her call they were evasive. It became evident that not only had the cottage not yet shed the aura of antipathy that had grown around it during the years, but that she herself was still regarded as an offender against their code. A few of the more kindly disposed women did venture to call but their edginess and haste to depart betrayed they had come from a sense of duty rather than to express condonation of her lapse in marrying Fergus. She could not bring herself to blame them. The stories of Fergus's misdemeanours continued to shock and outrage them and because they would never believe, supposing she ever disclosed them, the conditions of their marriage contract it was understandable that they must judge her as being inexcusably compliant.

She tried to console herself with work and, wanting it to be even more demanding, she suggested to Fergus that the croft could carry more animals and thus be made more profitable. His reply was an unintelligible grunt but several weeks later, without prior warning, the same stranger arrived and announced he had two in-calf heifers which Fergus had instructed him to deliver. While he was drinking the tea she offered the man observed smoothly, 'Fergus doesn't seem to manage to spend much of his time at home.'

'His fishing keeps him busy.' Her tone was expressionless.

'I'm thinking, seeing the size of his croft and the animals he now has, it must be a deal of work for a woman.'

She caught his furtive glance which told her that the sympathy in his voice was pretended; that he was simply testing her reaction in the hope of provoking her into an outburst against Fergus which he could then report to his companions. 'I manage well enough,' she assured him and, determined to give him no further opportunity to pry, took away his empty cup and plate. 'I mustn't keep you back,' she said with pointed civility.

It was true that she managed well enough without help from Fergus. She also managed, during the winter months, to join her neighbours in gathering winkles for dispatch to the mainland markets.

'My, but you're a hardy!' her neighbours commended her. 'All those beasts you have to see to and yet finding the strength to do this job. You'd best be watching you're not after killing yourself.'

She shrugged off their concern, edged, it seemed to her, with the implication that it was avarice that drove her to take on so much work. There were times when she wished she could tell them her true reason. The picking of winkles involved long hours of finger-freezing and back-breaking toil among the rocks and boulders of the shore for the duration of low tide, but the satisfying outcome for Anna was that it brought her money which, without mentioning it to Fergus, she could put by in the small shortbread tin which she kept in her clothes chest. She had begun her hoard with no specific purpose other than of having a degree of financial independence, money to make small purchases from the tinkers when they called, money to buy an occasional pair of shoes or perhaps, some day, a hat from the mail-order catalogue; but as Fergus's behaviour continued to embitter her, as he became ever more grudging in the provision of money for housekeeping, a vague idea began to form that one day, when she had sufficient savings, she might be able to gather her courage and dare to sever all connection with him and with the croft. She would never again be able to come back to the village since, no matter how much her marriage to Fergus had been disapproved of, rejecting the marriage would be, in the eyes of her neighbours, a more heinous crime. The thought that some day she might escape sustained her as, with scraped and bleeding fingers she tumbled boulders to get at the winkles underneath; it helped ease the ache of her bent back and hardened her to withstand the icy thrust of the wind between her shoulderblades.

'Oh, I'm wanting the spring to come,' moaned her neighbours when, the incoming tide having driven them from their labours, they tried to flap warmth into their bodies and ease their backs into straightness. And Anna could only envy them.

Until she had come to live in Fergus's cottage she had always been impatient for the coming of spring, its long days of relative calm and short nights of dimness without darkness compensating for the extra work it brought – the annual cleaning and airing of the cottage, the washing of blankets beside the burn, the peat cutting and corn sowing and potato planting – but sharing a home with Fergus had made the advance of spring loom like a portent of danger and she could greet it with none of the lilting joyousness of old.

Spring meant more plentiful fishing, which brought Fergus back more frequently and more unpredictably; it meant more hours of suffering his sulks and snarls while they were compelled to share the labour of peat cutting and potato planting; more opportunities for him to sink any trace of light-heartedness with his bludgeoning irascibility. Spring allowed her so few chances of escaping him that at the first sign of its coming her thoughts tended to switch to anticipating the stark days of winter.

The only times when she could be reasonably sure of being alone were when she went, late in the evenings, to milk the cows which were out on the hill. Fergus had no liking for cattle, no idea of how to milk a cow and no relish for trudging the hills and moors save for the track which led to and from his moored boat. Safe from the likelihood of encountering him, she could wander at will, taking her time, while the sounds and scents of the evening did their best to help lull her frayed nerves.

She had been out milking one evening after a particularly distressing day with Fergus and, having found one of the in-calf heifers missing, she had gone in search of it, suspecting that it had made its way to some secluded spot where, away from the attentions of the rest of the herd, it could give birth to its calf. When she found the heifer the calf was already born and on its feet, nuzzling its mother's flank as it sought her teats while the mother licked it with loving guidance. Anna, touched as always by the sight and by the rapturous protectiveness of the mother, sat down on a clump of heather to watch as the calf, its small tail wagging ecstatically, at last found its mother's teats and began to suck, weakly at first and then with increasing strength. Within the hour the calf was sturdy enough to be driven home with its mother and Anna began the leisurely trek back to the croft.

Once the cow and calf were settled in the byre she returned

100

to the house where to her surprise she found the door wide open. On going inside she saw Fergus's trousers, jersey and seaboot socks in a heap on the floor beside the recess bed. The sound of his heavy snoring came from behind the curtain. She stood perplexed. Since he had been late going out to his boat that day she had assumed that he would not return until the morning, if then. Now she was faced with the decision as to whether she should cook a meal and leave it ready for him when he woke or whether she should not bother to light the lamp but simply seek her own bed and risk his bawling anger should he wake before she rose in the morning. As she listened to his snore her own tiredness caught up with her. She decided she would go to bed and risk his not waking, but before leaving the kitchen she picked up his clothes and draped them over a chair near the bed where he would see them easily when he rose.

The next morning she was up early so as to make sure that all was well with the cow and new calf before she had to begin preparing the porridge for Fergus's breakfast. He was asleep when she went out to the byre and still asleep when she returned from her inspection, and since his clothes remained draped over the chair she took it that he had not wakened during the night. Trying to make no sound that might disturb him, she crept about the kitchen hastening her preparations so she might have everything ready to set before him as soon as he showed signs of wakening. She was bending over the pan of porridge, stirring it with the spirtle, when she heard his series of waking yawns followed by sporadic grunting. Guessing he was rousing himself to a sitting position in the bed, she made even more haste with her cooking. The porridge was ready; the kettle was on the boil. Within seconds she could fill his porridge bowl, scald the tea and tell him his breakfast was ready. Another second or two and she could be out of the kitchen. She heard the bed curtain being pushed back. The effort caused him to belch deeply.

101

'I want a clean vest and underpants!' he demanded in a thick grating voice. 'Hand them over to me. Quick!'

Anna's irritation flared. She intensely disliked seeing him in his underwear since it seemed to force on her an intimacy which she was loth to allow. But she knew she must humour him and, dutifully moving the porridge pan onto the hob, she turned and knelt beside the lowest drawer of the chest and extracted the garments he had asked for. Trying not to look at him directly, she approached the bed, expecting him to be sitting up with his lower half hidden by the bed cover. But her lowered gaze saw his bare feet were on the floor, saw his bulging calves were bare. Involuntarily her gaze was drawn upwards. His legs were bare, his thighs, his torso. As her eyes met his she saw that he was standing before her completely and unashamedly naked. At her expression of open-mouthed incredulity his lips parted in leering, soundless laughter. For an instant she felt paralysed and then, flinging the clothes at him, she snapped, 'Take them!' She made a rush for the door but, reaching out, Fergus grasped her arm and pulled her firmly back so she fell against his body. 'How dare you!' she choked, twisting vainly in his grip. 'You are a cheat! A liar!' she gasped. 'You are worse than a beast!'

'What's wrong with you? Never seen a naked man before, is that it?' His eyes were bright with mockery.

'I have not.' Her voice grew to an unaccustomed shrillness as she continued to struggle against his grip. 'Neither have I any wish to see you, naked as you are. Let go my arm at once!' She tried to speak with all the dignity she could muster.

He loosened his grip and again she made for the door, but with one leap he was in front of her and thrusting her roughly aside.

'What's all the fuss about?' he questioned. 'Is it fearing or hoping you are that I want to be defiling your precious body?' He sniggered. 'I'm thinking it's hope, isn't it?'

Anna held herself proudly, looking straight at him and

102

trying to annihilate him with the contempt of her expression.

'You've no need to worry yourself,' he went on to assure her. 'I vowed to you I wouldn't touch you and you can believe me I'm not finding it over hard to stick to my vow.' His eyes swept her from head to toe. 'You kindle nothing in me,' he sneered. 'I find you about as attractive as a bowl of cold gruel, so you've nothing to fear. I've not touched you before so why would I want to do it now?'

He still kept his grip on her arm but she began to breathe a fraction more easily. Suddenly his grip loosened but, seizing her left arm, he pushed up her sleeve, baring the thin twisted wrist. 'D'you think I'd want to risk fathering a bairn that might be born crippled like yourself? No bloody fear! I make sure my women come from healthier stock than came from your father's loins.' He let her arm drop as if it had been a noxious thing but moved swiftly to station himself between her and the door.

Lacerated by his cruelty and the falseness of his aspersions, she retaliated, 'My father was strong and healthy as were his forebears.'

'He had a brother who died without wits and another who died without lungs,' he sneered.

'They were gassed, both of them, fighting in the war,' she blazed at him. And with an upsurge of pride she added cuttingly, 'Neither of them brought home a woman from foreign parts as your father did. One who behaved in such a queer way even the kindest of folks spoke of her as having the madness in her.'

He lunged at her and hit her then, a heavy blow on the side of the face with his clenched fist, and would have hit her again had not the first blow sent her reeling back against the water pails, knocking them over as she fell. She could feel the water soaking coldly through her skirts and, pulling herself up to her feet, tried to evade him and get to the door, but the attack had brought on a sensation of dizziness which, allied

103

to the smell of stale sweat from his body, overwhelmed her with nausea. She saw his arms still crooked aggressively, the fists still clenched, and, knowing she was powerless against him, she closed her eyes, fighting back her frightened sobs as she raised her arms to fend off the further blows she expected. They did not come and except for his heavy breathing there was silence. She opened her eyes.

'Will you move and let me out?' she said tonelessly. 'I need fresh air.'

She was faintly surprised when, with an attempted nonchalance, he moved aside. Immediately her hands were fumbling with the latch. With the door open and escape looming before her she paused and without looking at him said, 'It may interest you to know that my twisted arm is the result of an illness I had when I was but a wee bairn. It is no inherited defect.' The next instant she was burning with mortification for having allowed herself to be drawn by his taunting.

'I'm not interested, have I not made it plain enough?' he shouted after her, and as she banged the door shut she heard his guffaw of vulgar laughter. Gasping with terror and relief, she fled blindly towards the sanctuary of the byre, only to collide with the ample figure of Tina-Willy, the tinker, who was coming along the path, her blanket-wrapped pack slung over her shoulder.

'The Dear save us!' exclaimed the old tinker. 'Is it a ghost or a monster that you're taking fright at?'

Anna struggled to regain control of herself. It would not do to let Tina-Willy see the state she was in or the whole village would be likely to hear of it. She put her hands firmly on the tinker's shoulder. 'It is nothing,' she told her. 'But we cannot go into the house just now for my man is ... he is taking a good wash.' The lie did not come easily. 'He spilled tar all over himself and has had to strip off his clothes. He would not be pleased to see you as he is.' She was aware that

104

Tina-Willy was assessing her shrewdly; conscious of her eyes lingering a second too long on the cheek that was stinging from Fergus's blow. 'Come now,' Anna insisted, 'we will go to the byre and look there at what you have.'

In the byre she tried hard to express a convincing degree of interest in the tinker's pack.

'I have just paid for the hens' meal so I have very little money until my man gives me money from the fishing,' she said by way of excuse for selecting only one small cheap towel from the assortment of goods. 'I will buy more from you when you come next spring.' To her surprise and shame, the tinker, without further solicitation, began folding the goods and stuffing them back into her pack.

With mounting disquiet Anna realized that she would have to go into her bedroom to get money from the shortbread tin, a thing she had carefully avoided doing when Fergus was present. And that he was still there she knew since all the time she had been looking over the tinker's bundle she had been keeping a careful watch on the cottage. She ached for the tinker to go but, in her mother's time and later in her own and, latest of all, since she had come to live in Fergus's cottage, it was the custom, once Tina-Willy's pack had been inspected and the necessary purchases made, for the old woman to be invited to sit in the kitchen and take a cup of tea and a helping of girdle scone. Tina-Willy expected it and Anna wanted to continue the hospitality, but she first had to ensure that Fergus was no longer there. She had no fear that he would strike her in the presence of the tinker but she did fear that he would be openly aggressive towards her and that Tina-Willy, observing it, would relish reporting it.

'We must wait here until I see my man has finished cleaning himself,' she told the old woman, and as a result condemned herself to listen with forced composure to the colourful and bawdy stories of the exploits of Tina-Willy's confederates.

105

After long, nerve-stretched minutes Fergus emerged from the cottage wearing his oilskins. He took the path down to the shore and as soon as he was out of sight Anna led the tinker into the kitchen. Not wanting her to notice too much amiss she commented with affected concern on the pool of water on the floor. 'Look now at the mess the man has made with his washing! The room is like a duck pond.' She righted the empty water pails and stood them back in place. 'Surely he could have made no more mess had he been dipping the sheep in here.' While the kettle was coming to the boil she mopped at the wet floor, continuing to comment on it in an attempt to lull the old tinker's obvious curiosity.

Tina-Willy folded her arms across her large bosom. 'You should take my advice and keep an old gumboot handy with a couple of good stones in the foot of it,' the old tinker prescribed blandly, 'an' the next time such a thing happens you wait for him to go to sleep just and then you wake him by giving him a good clout on his nose with it.'

Anna's dismay at the old woman's perception of the truth battled with the absurdity of waking a man in such a fashion.

'He'll likely go wild an' give you another beatin' the first time an' maybe the second time an' even the third,' Tina-Willy went on. 'But you must be sure to keep on doin' it until he gets that he's afeared of going to sleep at all. I guarantee he'll learn better ways then. An' he'll learn to respect you,' she nodded conviction. 'That is the very words my old mother said to me when I got myself wed. "You have to make a man respect you," says she, "An' there's no better way of doing it that I know of." An' that's the truth of it. You try it, girl, an' good luck to you.' She lifted her mug of tea as if drinking a toast. 'Thanks to you,' she murmured.

Anna blinked rapidly. She felt tight-packed with so many emotions that laughter had to spill out of her. She had tried not to laugh for fear of offending the tinker but since laughter served to disguise her troubled feelings she made no more

106

effort to stifle it. It was some time before she could stop herself from laughing but unperturbed the tinker carried on eating and drinking.

'It seems a heavy enough punishment for spilling a couple of pails of water on the floor,' Anna countered, still trying to delude the tinker into thinking nothing much was amiss.

'Indeed, so it would be for that alone.' Tina-Willy slid her an enigmatic glance and Anna knew her attempts at bluffing had been wasted.

When she had finished her tea the tinker stood up ready to take her leave. 'You an' your mother before you make the best scones I ever tasted,' she complimented Anna. 'I'm sayin' it's lucky the man that has such a one for a wife.' She picked up her pack. 'I will see you next year if the Lord spares me,' she said, and, with a duchess-like nod, made her departure.

Once Tina-Willy was out of sight Anna rushed from the kitchen and went back to the byre where, finding a dry sack, she collapsed trembling onto the stone step, her knees drawn up tight to her body. Her laughter at the tinker's advice had relaxed her to a degree but it seemed to have left her more vulnerable. The events of the morning had imprinted themselves on her mind and, shuddering at the degradation, she covered her eyes as if trying to press out the vividly recurring vision of Fergus's naked body.

She had been speaking the truth when she admitted to never having seen a naked man before. Not even so much as a picture of one. The old medical dictionary which her father had occasionally consulted, and which she had several times browsed over, had shown no illustration of a totally nude figure of either sex, and the unexpected and close sight of Fergus's naked body, his muscular legs and strong thighs, his genitals insolently conspicuous among the screen of dark hair that looked coarser and blacker than the hair which covered so much of his body, had struck her as being grotesque, filling her with such repugnance that she had been on the brink of

107

screaming. Even now, as she pictured it, she had the sensation that a scream was threatening to burst from her throat. What had prompted him to display himself so flagrantly to her in the way he had? Since he had reiterated he had no designs on her, she came to the conclusion that he wanted only to shock her and that the incident had doubtless happened as the result of some ribald challenge made during a session of drinking with some of his lewder cronies.

The sun, which earlier had been only a deceptive rumour, burst from the sullen clouds to shine with sudden warmth and brilliance and, as if they had been impatiently awaiting its appearance, skylarks began to soar and descend, filling the air with their song. Slowly unfolding her taut body to the sun, Anna began to blame herself that her reaction to Fergus's provocation had been too extreme. Why had she been so shaken by the sight of his nakedness? Why had she allowed him to see how disturbed she had been? Why, at her age, could she not have turned from him with a shrug of contempt and a caustic word of dismissal before walking calmly out of the kitchen?

Cooling the palms of her hands on the stone step, she held them against her hot brow. Gently her fingers slid over her bruised and swollen cheek. She disavowed blame. I hate him, she told herself implacably. I hate him. When I agreed to marry him I had no liking for him, but neither had I hate. In all my life I have not known how to hate, but he has taught me as no one else could have done. The intensity of her emotion startled her and, as if to justify it, she again went over the scene of the morning. Fergus had deliberately shamed her by exposing himself. He had degraded her and her family by his aspersions and he had attacked her viciously when she had tried to evade him. Reason argued that when she had been at his mercy he had made no attempt to ravish her. That he had indeed reaffirmed his lack of interest in her. And yet, irrationally, the knowledge brought no comfort.

Her body felt as if it had been violated and then spurned. The quivering hollowness inside her took some minutes for her to comprehend and shamed her when she did so. Abhorrence was quick to reassert itself. With a whimper of resignation she again drew up her knees, letting her head droop to rest on her folded arms while she tried to expunge the persistent image of Fergus's nakedness from her mind.

10

Two days passed without Fergus putting in an appearance and during that time Anna was bolstering up her courage to face him. When on the third evening, while she was scalding the mash for the hens, he stumped into the kitchen she was ready for him. 'Fergus McFee...' she began bluntly, giving him no time to put down the pail he was carrying or to divest himself of oilskins before she spoke, 'I am telling you now that if you ever again behave as you did the other morning I shall be leaving this house on the instant.'

'I shall behave as I like in my own home,' he blustered, though, to Anna, his defiance sounded to have a touch of the bogus about it. 'Anyway, what's upsetting you about what I did? Haven't I made it clear enough I have no fancy for you? How many times will I have to tell you before you'll give up the idea?'

She let the innuendo pass. 'You struck me,' she accused him. Her hand went up to her still bruised tender cheek.

'You taunted me and made me lose my temper.' His voice took on an edge of savageness. 'Anyway, haven't I struck you before and you've taken it meek enough, so what's upsetting you about this last time?' He was looking directly at her, his teeth bared in a mocking smile.

'You know full well what I am speaking about,' she

retorted. Her eyes regarded him unflinchingly; her voice stayed firm. 'And I am meaning what I say. If such a thing happens again I will no longer remain in this house.'

He began to laugh outright, swaying back on his heels, deriding her as she stood facing him, only the nervous clasping and unclasping of her hands revealing the ferment inside her. 'All that bloody fuss over seeing a naked man,' he scoffed. 'I'm thinking there's likely a lot more wrong with you than a twisted hand. Maybe your mind is twisted too.' He tipped a pail of live crabs onto the table. 'Get those roasted!' he commanded. 'I'm hungry.' He turned away without seeing the withering look she gave him before picking up the crabs and beginning to prepare them.

Although Anna could not completely convince herself that her threat to leave him had effectively safeguarded her from Fergus, there was no recurrence of the scene which had so upset her. However, there was a noticeably increasing malevolence in his attitude towards her. He began to shout more loudly, to swear more obscenely, to find fault more readily, and to take every chance of elbowing her out of his way more roughly. He deliberately subjected her to other aggravations. Frequently when she came inside she would find the water pails, which she had left full, quite empty, necessitating a hasty visit to the well to refill them before she could brew tea or even have a drink of water to quench her thirst. There were times when washing she had put out on the dykes to bleach in the sun would be unaccountably soiled. Times when calf tethers which she had hammered firmly into the ground had been loosened, allowing the calves to pull them up and wander, so that she was compelled to go in search of them. Suspecting that Fergus was trying to goad her into active protest with the idea of giving himself reason for treating her even more abusively, she gritted her teeth against him, enclosing herself in a kind of carapace off which the barbs of his hostility glanced and under which she became so

111

insensitive to his bullying that her consciousness ceased to register the increasing degree of her loathing for him.

On only two subsequent occasions did she allow herself to be driven into betraying signs of rage against her husband.

Returning from the hill one autumn evening after the milking she was startled to see smoke rising from a corner of the croft. Since Fergus had left in his boat quite late in the afternoon she was not expecting him to return until at least the early hours of the morning and her first thought on seeing the smoke was that it was likely to be the result of some camper who had carelessly set fire to a clump of heather while lighting his camping stove. She scanned it with narrowed eyes. It did not look like heather smoke. With rising apprehension she put down the milk pails and ran to investigate. Within a hundred yards of the fire she slowed her approach. Only the easily recognizable figure of Fergus stood beside the fire and the moment he saw her he immediately lifted a can of paraffin and fed the reluctant flames. They blazed up and she ran forward, her hand clutching at her throat, stifling her cry of anguish when she saw the charred pages of her precious books swirling into blackened fragments as they were lifted by the breeze.

A pitchfork lay on the ground a little distance away and, rushing forward, she seized it and began raking desperately at the remnants of hard covers and pages that showed signs of surviving the flames. With a snarled oath Fergus thrust her aside, wresting the fork from her as he did so.

'I'll teach you to waste your time when I'm away,' he threatened as he gloatingly pushed the books into the centre of the fire.

'You fiend!' she screamed at him, and dodged away as he swung round with the pitchfork raised as if he was about to strike her. She saw his face contorted with hatred before he turned his attention once again to the fire. For a few

112

moments she stood rigid with despair, her arms folded tightly across her chest, her eyes riveted on the vengeful destruction. The sudden realization that Fergus must have gone into her bedroom to find her books spurred her to action and she raced back to the house, praying on sobbing breaths that he had not broken into her clothes chest and found the secret hoard of money in the shortbread tin. The door of her bedroom was open but the chest, covered by a cloth on which reposed her mother's Bible, looked undisturbed. Not trusting what she saw, she went down on her knees, and feverishly inserting the key into the lock, lifted the lid. The contents too looked untampered with and, almost unnerved by the extent of her relief, she lifted out the shortbread tin. It rattled reassuringly. Opening it she counted the coins. There was none missing. Either he had not suspected she had such a hoard or she had returned in time to thwart his further investigations. She clasped the tin to her chest, telling herself she must think of a safer place to conceal it. She must never again assume that Fergus would respect her possessions, never risk his discovering the tin.

Following the burning of the books the timidly nursed hopes of one day being able to leave her husband had crystallized into a fierce resolve, and it was the contents of the tin, to which she must continue to add, that would provide the means for her to achieve it.

Her plan was simple. Before she had thrown in her lot with Fergus and when she had been trying to find work, her schoolteacher friend had urged her to spend a few weeks' holiday with her and her mother at their home in the south of England, suggesting that it would be fairly easy for her to find work there and that, if nothing else was available, her semi-invalid mother would be glad of a companion help. Had Anna been able to do so she would have gladly accepted the invitation but, unable to afford the fare for the long

113

journey and too proud to admit it, she had given some reason for being unable to avail herself of the offer. The invitation from her friend had been renewed frequently and always with increasing cordiality, but though Anna had longed to accept she knew she had little hope of ever being able to do so. Suddenly the prospect seemed not so remote as she had imagined it to be. By the end of the coming winter she reckoned that with the money she could expect to earn from whelk picking she should have enough saved not only to pay her fare but also to leave a small sum for extras. After that she could only hope her friend's prediction about finding work still held some substance. But whatever happened she would not come back here, she vowed. She would never see Fergus again. Never! Never!

That winter excelled itself in the ferocity of the gales which at nearly every low tide drove the would-be whelk gatherers pitilessly from their work. Time and time again Anna tried stoically to disregard the menace of the breaking swell which threatened to sweep her off her feet and into the wildly foaming sea. Time after time she tried to ignore the wind-driven deluges of rain slanting at her like massed arrows and piercing the armour of her clothing until, soaked to the skin and so cold she could barely move, she had to abandon the whelks and return home with sometimes a bare pailful instead of the two to three sackfuls she had been expecting to pick. Before the winter was halfway over she realized that there would be little to add to her hoard in the shortbread tin and her plan would have to wait until after yet another winter.

The long winter evenings without the consolation of her books drove her at times near to despair. Reading had always been such a passion with her that there were moments when she felt goaded to rifle the contents of the shortbread tin for the purpose of sparing a little to replace one or two of the books she most missed. Had she been able to go into a shop and buy them she might have come perilously close to doing so, but the composing of the letter, the purchasing of a postal order, and then the posting of the letter so protracted the decision that she was saved from having to make it. She concentrated on her knitting but, since she had invariably knitted and read at the same time, plying her needles without a book open on her lap seemed to intensify her loss. She composed herself to darn and redarn Fergus's hated socks and underwear. She mended clothes which even in her parents' frugal household would have been discarded as being beyond repair. So as to save spending money on herself she resorted to making her nightdresses and underwear out of the bleached cotton flour sacks which hitherto she had been accustomed to use only for teatowels. The material was coarse but it softened with repeated washing, so, much as she would have liked to buy less austere garments from the mail-order catalogues or even from Tina-Willy's pack, she forbade herself from being tempted, smug in the knowledge that such economies would hasten the day of her liberation.

The spring brought Tina-Willy on her annual visit and once Anna had bought the minimum that would satisfy the old tinker and had settled her down to her usual tea and gossip, the old woman asked, 'D'you mind a gentleman by the name of James Cameron? Lives overby at Cruachan?'

'James Cameron?' Anna mused. 'No,' she said vaguely, 'I cannot remember ever having being acquainted with anyone of that name.'

'Well, he was askin' after you very kindly. Wantin' to know if you still lived hereabouts.'

'Asking after me?' Anna interrupted. 'Are you sure?'

'Aye, indeed. He says he was after meetin' you when you was no more than a young lassie at school. He told me he was a bit of a wanderer in those days and pickin' up a livin'

115

here and there mostly doin' a bit of mussel pearlin'. He was sayin' you took pity on him and brought him over a good meal of fresh scones and crowdie.'

'Jimmy Pearl!' exclaimed Anna. 'Could that be who you are speaking of?'

'Indeed, I daresay that's what folks might have called him in those days,' replied the tinker. 'But Mester James Cameron he is now an' as well thought of as the minister himself.'

'I remember Jimmy Pearl, certainly,' Anna admitted. 'But I never knew him by any other name. So he is James Cameron, is he? How strange it is to be hearing of him again after such a brief encounter so many years ago. Stranger too that he should have remembered me...' She broke off. 'Wait now,' she bade the tinker. 'He gave me something then which I shall show you.' Going into her bedroom she delved in her clothes chest for the matchbox containing the pearls. 'See,' she said, returning to the kitchen, 'I've managed to keep these safe and they're as pretty now as on the day he gave them to me.' Sliding open the box, she displayed the pearls. It was the first time she had shown them to anyone save her mother.

Tina-Willy, leaning forward to inspect them, made a suitably admiring comment. 'He's no likely to be needin' to go mussel pearlin' again,' she said. 'Like as not he could buy plenty of pearls if he wanted them,' she added significantly.

'I've sometimes wondered what happened to him,' Anna said. 'I never expected to hear of him again.'

'What happened, so he told me, is that he and a friend of his made it up to go together to Australia or Canada or some other foreign place I don't remember, where they'd heard tell there was good money to be made by people just wandering around from place to place like what they were keen on doin'. Prospectin' I think they were, an' it seems they was doin' pretty well for themselves until his friend was injured in an accident of some sort and decided he'd be better off coming back to Scotland to be with his folks. Mester Cameron

116

himself stayed on and went on farmin' for a teen of years till he reckoned he'd made enough an' it was time to come back. He's been back now a couple of years or more. An' he's got a good croft over in Cruachan an' is as settled as ever a man can be, I reckon.'

'I remember him as being a nice gentlemanly young man,' Anna observed. 'And I'm glad to know he's done well enough for himself even if he didn't achieve what his parents had planned for him.' Catching Tina-Willy's look of inquiry, she explained. 'He was said to be a fine scholar and expected to do well in some profession. A minister I believe they wanted him to be. People said he showed such promise he could have gone far if he'd had a mind to do so.'

'A minister, indeed?' queried Tina-Willy. 'Ach, but he hasn't the eyes of a minister.' Puzzled, Anna glanced at her. 'He has the joy of this world in his eyes, not the next,' interpreted the tinker. 'But he's a gentleman, right enough. A gentleman in every way, I'd say, an' it takes a tinker or a duke to know a real gentleman when they're met with.'

'Has he a family?' Anna asked with only conventional interest.

'Not that I've set eyes on,' replied Tina-Willy. 'He's never made any mention to my ears of a family. He lives by himself just an' with an old widow woman an' her son glad to come an' help him when he needs help.'

'Well, I'm pleased to know he has remembered me,' Anna said as Tina-Willy rose and shouldered her pack. 'And when you next see him I hope you will kindly tell him from me I still have the pearls he gave me.' For a few moments a tenderly reminiscent smile hovered around her lips, only to vanish instantly as the noise of thudding boots came from outside. The old tinker, hearing Anna's sharp intake of breath and seeing her thrust the matchbox quickly into the pocket of her apron, immediately took in the situation.

'Is that your man back?'

Anna nodded, tight-lipped and strained.

'I'd best be away,' said the tinker.

Fergus pushed rudely past her into the kitchen. 'Out of my way!' To Anna he growled, 'You get rid of her pretty quick!'

Tina-Willy stood her ground. 'An' what like of a man is it that would be wantin' to drive a poor harmless tinker out of his house in such a coarse way,' she remonstrated.

'Be off with you!' Fergus ordered. 'You're nothing but a plague around the place.'

The old tinker, boldly facing him, drew herself up to her full height. The hand that was not holding her pack was akimbo on her hip as her contemptuous glance appraised him. 'If I were not a lady I would spit on you,' she declared before turning her back on him and sweeping majestically out of the house.

Fergus bounded to the door. 'Don't you come back here!' he shouted after her. He turned to Anna. 'If I find her here again I'll lay hands on her and throw her out,' he warned.

Anna was not much surprised when Tina-Willy, heedless of Fergus's threats, turned up at the cottage the following spring. What surprised her was that the old tinker handed her an envelope addressed simply to 'Anna Matheson'. The letter inside was signed 'James Cameron'.

'So, you still have the wee pearls I gave you, Anna,' he had written.

So no doubt you remember your flying leap over the crag when you almost landed in my dinner? You see, I too have my memories. Never since that time have I tasted such excellent girdle scones and crowdie. No, not anywhere in the world, of which I have seen a good deal since you wished me *Beannachd leat!* and skipped off barefooted over the heather.

You will no doubt have learned from our mutual friend Tina-Willy (what a character the old lady is!) that I have settled on a croft in Cruachan and if you are ever visiting nearby you will be very welcome to call on me. Tina-Willy will, I am sure, give a good

118

good account of me and I daresay I shall be able to offer you food that will be more to your liking than that which I was able to offer in those long ago days of our meeting.

Should I ever have the good fortune to find myself in the vicinity of your home I take it that I shall be equally welcome to call on you and your man? It would be good to talk over what became of your ambitions and of mine (if I had such things in those days!). It would be good too to have the prospect of sampling girdle scones made by your own good self in the expectation that you have inherited your mother's skill at making them. Tina-Willy assures me this is so.

Blessings on your house and health and happiness be yours.

Your once encountered acquaintance,

James Cameron

Anna, greatly touched that he should have written to her in such a friendly way, tried to bring his image back to her mind as she went about her work. She could not truthfully pretend that her meeting with Jimmy Pearl, as she still thought of him, had left any deep and lasting impression on her, but on the other hand she had not dismissed it entirely from her memory. Until she had married Fergus, when even phantom images of happiness had been driven to flight, the scene of their encounter had in quiet moments flashed fitfully across her mind. She began trying to picture him as he had looked then, polishing up her impression of him, and wondered if, were they to meet casually, either of them would recognize the other. It seemed to her unlikely, but she knew that should she ever chance to be near Cruachan she would most certainly wish to call on him.

She read the letter through again that evening and as she did so a finger of dismay tweaked at her pleasure in receiving it. He mentioned calling on her if he was in the area and this she must somehow dissuade him from doing. She could not bear that he should see the mean appearance of the place she now called home or that he should gain an inkling of the thankless conditions under which she was compelled to labour. Least of all could she bear him to witness her subjection should he call when Fergus was present.

11

For some weeks she considered how she should word her response to Jimmy Pearl's letter and was sitting at the kitchen table composing what at last she had concluded was a suitable reply when she heard a man's voice hailing her from outside. Quickly she slipped the letter into her apron pocket and went to the door. It was with some foreboding she found herself confronted by the man whom she now knew as Mac and who had on two previous occasions brought cattle which Fergus had bought. Not more cows, her thoughts resisted instantly. Not only could she not cope with more cows but the official souming for the croft had already been reached and there would likely be complaints if it was exceeded.

After a polite but perfunctory greeting Mac said, 'There's a horse out at the back there.' Inclining his head towards the byre, he added, 'Fergus said I was to bring it.' He seemed strangely ill at ease.

'A horse?' Anna exclaimed in astonishment. 'Whose horse?'

'I reckon it's Fergus's horse, right enough, seein' he bought it at the sale,' he rejoined.

'Fergus bought a horse and told you to bring it here?' Anna felt dazed with incredulity. 'Are you sure this is right what you are telling me?'

'Indeed I am so.'

121

'Did he tell you what purpose he had in buying the horse?' She knew it was a useless question. Fergus rarely told anyone about his motives for doing anything.

'He did not. All I know is Fergus was that keen to get the horse he paid more than enough for it.'

Anna scanned Mac's face closely, suspecting he might be playing some joke on her. 'Why in the Dear's name would he be wanting to buy a horse?' Her question was directed as much to herself as to Mac. 'Fergus doesn't know the first thing about horses,' she added. 'I'm certain of that.'

Mac's unease increased. 'I was surprised myself,' he admitted. 'I would never have expected Fergus to buy a horse.' He appeared to be considering what more he could say and then, as if with sudden resolution, he became confidential. 'I believe it might have been this way. See, Fergus had this grudge against the fellow who was havin' to sell the horse.' He glanced furtively at Anna before resuming; 'Maybe you heard that Fergus at one time wanted to marry a lassie from the port by the name of Catriona McLeod?' He cocked an embarrassed eye at her. Anna raised a disinterested eyebrow. 'Fergus was awful fond of Catriona at one time,' Mac went on, 'but she chose to marry a fellow called Andrew Nicholson. Fergus was pretty mad about it at the time as you'd expect an' he took to tauntin' Andrew no end whenever he got the chance. My, but the two worked up a right hatred for each other an' I believe it was disappointment over Catriona an' his hate for Andrew that set Fergus off drinkin' an' lookin' for other woman.' Recollecting himself, he hastened to explain, 'In the past I was meanin', before he was married.' Anna remained indifferent. 'Well, Catriona died sudden a year or two back an' you'd never believe how Fergus blamed Andrew for it. Andrew was that shaken by it all he got that he didn't seem to care any more what happened to him. He let everything go, just, his croft, his cows an' his sheep. The change in him was terrible to see an' he started goin' to pubs where you'd never have seen him when Catriona was alive. Ach, it was a shame right enough. The man was killin' himself with not eatin' an' not bein' used to the drink. Folks said the only reason he didn't do away with himself was because he had this horse. Right enough he seemed to care a lot for this horse.' Mac paused and pursed his lips as if suddenly regretful that he had said so much.

'Why, since there was so much hate between them, did Andrew allow Fergus, of all people, to get his hands on the horse?'

'To my mind Fergus was the last person Andrew would have wanted to have it,' Mac told her. 'But he was in hospital with his stomach and, from the look of him last time I saw him, he's not likely to come out again.' Mac shrugged his shoulders in what was obviously an expression of sympathy. 'He would never have been able to keep the horse anyway seein' he'd have been sold up for owin' so much money around the place.'

'But if, as you say, Fergus had such a grudge against Andrew why would he have been so keen to buy his horse?' Anna demanded to know. For a fleeting moment she wished Mac might attribute a grain of compassion to Fergus but even as the wish formed it was displaced by the suspicion that Fergus's motive was more likely to have been a harsh one. Mac seemed to be struggling to tell her something he wished he did not feel compelled to divulge. 'What would you say was the reason for it?' Anna pressed.

'Ach, some men have strange ways of bearin' a grudge,' he mumbled evasively.

Just as she was on the point of arguing that Fergus was far too tight-fisted to continue bearing a grudge up to the point when it cost him money to do so, Mac said, 'Maybe I shouldn't be sayin' what I am sayin' but Fergus isn't one that likes to be crossed an' gettin' at a horse might please him as

123

well as gettin' at Andrew.' He shot her a glance of sly inquiry. 'You'll maybe understand what I'm thinkin'?'

The significance of what he was hinting at suddenly smote her. Her face set. 'I'd best go and take a look at the horse,' she said.

Still smouldering over the thought that Fergus had contrived to thrust even more responsibility on her shoulders, she followed Mac towards the byre. Looking after a horse was exclusively a task for the male members of a family. Anna had never had any experience of tending horses. Indeed, she had been brought up to regard a horse as a luxury since it brought in no income and was of negligible benefit to the croft. These disadvantages she determined to point out to Fergus, stressing, at the same time, that they had managed well enough up to now without the help of a horse. She would tell him too that if he was expecting a horse to work he must also expect to feed it and that feeding a horse meant there would be less hay for a more productive animal. She reasoned that once he knew what keeping a horse entailed his mean spirit would prompt him to sell the animal just as soon as he could find a buyer.

'That's her over there!' Mac exclaimed as they came round the byre.

A mare! Anna just managed not to voice her surprise but she was aware of the quick catch of her breath as she stared at the horse standing serenely beside the fence post to which it was roped. She could see immediately that it was not the rough hill pony she had expected it to be.

'She's nice an' she's that gentle I hadn't one bit of trouble bringin' her over. A real lady I'd say she is.' Anna, still intent on the horse, was only half aware that Mac was speaking to her. 'Will I loose her?' he asked. She murmured assent.

At Mac's approach the horse turned its head and looked, not at him, but directly at her. Its ears pricked and it seemed to Anna that its attention was entirely on her. The moment it

124

was free, as if bidden, the horse walked towards her with such confidence that she formed the impression it had mistaken her for someone it thought it recognized. Though she had never before been so close to a horse she felt curiously unafraid when the mare, pausing in front of her, blew gently into her face. As she reached up to stroke between its ears the mare took the opportunity to nuzzle under her chin and blow in her ear. Anna was aware of a swift sense of rapport between her and the mare. She continued caressing its head.

'What did Andrew call her?' she asked. She thought it unlikely that the mare had been given a name. It was not the practice to allow horses the distinction of a name. They were referred to and called simply *Ech* which was the Gaelic word for horse.

'I believe Andrew called her Solas,' Mac disclosed. 'Folks did say he called her that because he got her just before Catriona died, though I wouldn't be sure of that myself.'

Solas! It was the Gaelic word for solace and even after such a brief acqaintance Anna had the feeling that the mare might have been aptly named. 'She's nice!' Anna echoed Mac's inadequate approval and, not wanting him to perceive how much she admired the horse, she said briskly, 'I'll get some hay for her to eat while you come to the house and take a cup of tea.'

When Mac had taken his leave Anna went out again to the horse. 'You are indeed a lady,' she told the mare which, having finished its feed of hay, submitted itself to Anna's attention. 'I'm not surprised Andrew was fond of you.' She patted the mare's smooth neck and rested her head against its shoulder. 'Solas,' she murmured, and the thought occurred that, improbable as it would once have seemed, she, who had never had the remotest interest in horses, was now asking herself if the mare might not be destined to bring some degree of solace into her own desolate life.

When Fergus came home she waited for him to mention

125

the horse and to give her some idea of his intentions. She waited in vain and when, after a few days' absence, he returned again and still made no mention of the horse she began to wonder whether he had indeed bought it; whether he had done so but had given Mac the wrong instructions for its delivery; whether he had been so drunk at the sale that he had completely forgotten the transaction. If that was so she prayed his forgetfulness might continue. The horse would fare better without his attention. She had begun to think of Solas as her own secret possession, but the next time he came home he demanded, 'Where's the horse I bought? I've not seen it around.'

'It is away on the hill with the other horses,' she told him with assumed indifference.

He made a disgruntled comment which she did not catch and then said forcefully, 'See she stays there till I need her.'

Anna washed and put away the dishes with less speed than usual, giving him the chance to enlighten her as to why he had acquired the horse, but he remained silent. Slumping down in his chair, he took a netting needle from his pocket and began repairing some of his creel nets; anxious as she was to know his intentions towards Solas, she decided it was best not to question him.

As the weeks passed she began to worry more and more over the welfare of the mare. Neighbours who were more familiar with horses had assured her that Solas would do well enough out on the hill during the summer and early autumn, but they were insistent that the mare was not sturdy enough to be outwintered as were the rest of the horses. She was too fine they warned, assessing the mare's build, and she would most certainly need the shelter of a stable on winter nights and good feeding if she was to survive.

Recognizing that she passionately desired the mare to remain in her care and fearing that if she passed on the warnings to Fergus he would immediately send Solas to the sale, she kept the information to herself. It would be up to her to devise some way of ensuring the horse was housed and fed in the cold weather. When she thought about it, her own fondness for the mare mystified her. In the past it had not been unusual for her to become attached to some particular cow or calf in her care but it had always been an expedient affection, never complicated by sentiment, and a good price at the sale had invariably proved ample compensation for parting with any animal. But Solas had come to mean so much to her that she resolved, whatever the cost, not to allow Fergus to outwinter the mare, which, she suspected, was his intention. There would be no trouble about housing the mare when Fergus was not at home but she did not look forward to the scenes that might ensue on the nights when he was at home. She comforted herself by hoping and praying that the winter would be wild enough to keep him in the port harbour.

Yet another surprise awaited her when she returned to the house after milking and found the local carrier awaiting her. He had brought a cart, he told her, but he had left it at the far end of the croft because the track was too rough to get his lorry any nearer the house. Her heart sank at the news. So Fergus was intending harnessing Solas to a cart! She wondered if the horse had ever known a harness; wondered what her reaction would be if it was attempted; wondered if Fergus had ever handled a horse and cart. He continued to keep her in ignorance of his plans and because she feared to let him see how much she cared for the horse she continued to ask no questions.

When the winter frosts set in she began bringing Solas into one of the sheds at night and giving her a feed of bran and hay. She was coming away from stabling the mare one evening when Fergus appeared. Swallowing the dryness that immediately afflicted her throat, she faced him defiantly.

'You'll make that beast soft,' Fergus accused truculently.

127

'She is soft,' Anna replied. 'Too soft to be left out in weather like this. It would kill her and the money you paid for her would be wasted.' Since there would be no further sales until the summer and since no one would wish to buy a horse they would have to house and feed all winter, she felt safe in reminding him that losing the horse would result in his losing money, and when he made no further objection she experienced a satisfying sense of victory.

It was not until after the New Year that Fergus announced, 'I'm thinking of slaughtering a sheep or two and hawking them around on the horse and cart. The old fellow that's been doing it up till now says he cannot carry on any longer.'

His announcement startled and dismayed her. They could spare the sheep but how would Solas take to dragging a cart from house to house? How long might the mare be left standing in the cold outside some house or hotel while Fergus lingered inside? 'Has the horse ever been between shafts?' she asked him.

'If she hasn't she'll learn soon enough,' was his reply.

She wanted to protest further but knew that for the mare's sake she must not pursue the matter.

Fergus commanded that it must be she who selected the best sheep for slaughtering and demanded her presence while he wielded the knife. Inured since childhood to the killing and butchering of sheep for the household meat supply, she attended dutifully, holding the pail ready to catch the blood which she would later make into black pudding.

When he considered the carcasses had hung for a sufficient length of time Fergus required her help to wrap the joints in the ubiquitous flour sacks, ready to be loaded onto the cart.

'Get the horse!' he ordered peremptorily. She saw then why he made no objection when he had discovered she was stabling Solas at night. To have had to go out to the hill to search for the mare or, as was more likely, to have had to send her to search for it, would have delayed the start of his meat

128

round. Reluctantly she went to the stable and brought out Solas. As soon as the mare saw Fergus she stood still, her nostrils quivering as if she scented danger. Fergus came and took hold of the bridle. The horse snorted and tried to shy away. Fergus swore. 'What's wrong with the beast?' he roared at Anna.

'I think perhaps she can smell the raw meat on your hands,' Anna said. 'Animals are said to be upset by it.'

'Well, she can bloody well get used to it!' He pulled and twisted the bridle and the horse tried desperately to free herself.

Anna turned to go back to the house, not wanting to watch his further attempts at manoeuvring the horse between the shafts.

'Come back here, you daft creature!' Fergus bellowed after her. 'You'll need to give me a hand to steady her once I've got the beast where I want her.'

It soon became obvious to Anna that Solas had never previously been between shafts and that Fergus had no knowledge of how to go about the task of putting her there. Helplessly she was forced to watch the struggle as Fergus, becoming more and more infuriated, tried to kick and punch and bully the frenzied horse into subjection. Several times Anna cried out to him to spare the horse but her cries went unheeded, and when she tried to intervene by pulling at his arm a blow with his clenched fist knocked her to her knees.

At last Solas was between the shafts, sweating and trembling, eyes rolling and mouth foaming. 'Now you come here and hold on to the beast while I load the cart!' Fergus ordered. Feeling traitorous and ashamed, Anna did as she was bidden, taking the opportunity when Fergus's back was turned to whisper soothingly to the horse and to stroke her quivering neck in an effort to calm her agitation.

'Now you can lead her up to the road,' Fergus directed. 'First I must get a blanket for you to throw over the horse should you have to leave it standing in the cold,' she insisted. She expected to hear his derisive refusal but he seemed so taken aback by her temerity in opposing him that he waited while she ran to the stable for the horse blanket which she had made by sewing together old meal sacks. She placed the folded blanket on the cart. 'You will not forget what I told you. You will be without your money and without your meat round if anything happens to the horse,' she reminded him.

'Shut your mouth!' he retorted. 'And get leadin' that horse.'

She led Solas with a gentle hand on the bridle but as soon as they reached the road, with a cry of 'Let go!', Fergus raised his whip and cracked it so close above the horse's back that Anna felt it lift the strands of her own hair. Solas responded by rearing on her hind legs before jerking forward and racing madly along with the cart clattering behind her as she bolted along the road. She had not got far before Anna saw something fall of the back of the cart and when she went to retrieve it she found it was the horse blanket. 'He's mad!' she sobbed to herself. 'Quite, quite mad!' Fervently she prayed that no harm would come to the horse.

She had three days to fret over Solas's welfare before Fergus returned from the meat round, arriving late on a pitch-black night of piercingly cold wind which brought frequent showers of mingled sleet and hail. As usual the smell of drink enveloped him and as he threw off his oilskins he swayed against the doorframe. She guessed he would not have stabled Solas but, without a word, she set his meal before him and while he was eating it she lit the hurricane lamp and prepared to put on her waterproof. Fergus looked blearily at her.

'Where d'you think you're going?' he demanded to know.

'I'm going to stable the horse since I take it you have not done so,' she said.

Jumping up, Fergus lurched towards her and snatched the lamp from her grasp. 'That horse can stay out on the hill for

130

all the use it is,' he barked at her. 'There's no call for it to be eating it's head off inside. I doubt if I'll be wanting it again anyway.'

'The horse needs shelter if it needs nothing else,' she tried to argue.

He swung the lamp threateningly. 'Get you off to your bed,' he told her. 'I want you out of my sight.' He banged the lamp down on the table.

Anna picked it up and blew it out. 'There's no use burning paraffin when it's not needed then, is there?' she dared to point out and, replacing the lamp on its usual hook in the porch, she went through to her bedroom. She did not undress but sat on her bed listening for sounds from the kitchen. She expected soon to hear him throw himself down on the recess bed but it seemed a long time before there was any movement at all. It began to seem as if he had fallen asleep in his chair as he sometimes did and she would have to wait goodness knows how long before he woke sufficiently to realize he was not in his bed. And all this time Solas would be exposed to the weather! The thought chafed at her mind. Suddenly she heard a thump and guessed that in waking Fergus had tipped over his chair. She heard him cursing and then a few moments later she heard more thumps as he flung himself onto his bed. Knowing he would soon fall into a drunken sleep, she listened for him to begin snoring and allowed him to snore for some time before she opened her bedroom door and crept noiselessly into the porch. Throwing her waterproof over her shoulders and reaching for the hurricane lamp, she went outside and made her way through the turbulent darkness to the stable where it was safe to light the lamp.

She guessed that Solas, instead of making for the hill when Fergus had abandoned her, would have waited only for him to disappear in the direction of the house before making for her stable and that, finding the stable door closed, she would then wisely have made for the nearest shelter which, with the

131

wind in its present direction, Anna knew would be in the lee of the byre. Not daring to call out, Anna lifted the lamp high, shielding the wind-threatened flame as she tried to peer through the darkness. 'Solas!' she breathed with relief as she discerned the dark shape of the horse standing close pressed against the stone wall. 'You poor creature. Come now into the dry.' The horse followed her eagerly into the stable where there was fresh, dry bedding and a manger full of hay.

In the lamplight Solas looked a sadly different horse from the one which had set out three days ago. Her ears were flat against her head; her coat was so sodden that the rain still dripped from it. Grabbing some dry sacks, Anna rubbed the mare down vigorously, murmuring endearments and commiserations while she did so. Noticing Solas flinch as the sack touched certain spots on her back, Anna brought the lamp closer and saw the telltale weals. The sight so much angered her that she longed to rush and inflict similar hurt on Fergus. Recklessly she wondered whether, had she dared earlier to carry out the advice Tina-Willy had given her, she might by now have ensured Fergus's respect for herself and consequently for the horse. But it was useless to envisage doing it now. It was no longer just herself who was vulnerable to his bullying: there was also Solas on whom he would not hesitate to wreak his revenge. 'He's mad, Solas,' she confided to the horse. 'He's mad and bad and I fear and hate him!'

Above the sound of the storm she heard a different noise and, suspecting it might be Fergus, was gripped so tightly by apprehension that she hardly allowed herself to breathe. The horse had heard it too and, as if Anna's fear had immediately communicated itself, the mare moved restlessly, disregarding the hay in her manger as she turned her head towards the door. Anna continued to listen but the noise identified itself as a corner of the roof creaking as the changing wind buffeted it. Anna breathed more easily. 'It's all right, Solas,' she was able to reassure the horse. 'We're safe. It's not himself.' But it

132

was several tense minutes before her qualms completely abated and before Solas resumed eating her hay.

When she was satisfied that Solas was as dry as she could rub her, Anna rugged the mare with more sacks. She would have dearly liked to have given her a warm mash before leaving her for the night but without risking waking Fergus she had no access to hot water.

'Goodnight, Solas!' she bade the horse after a last scrutiny. 'There'll be a good warm mash for you as soon as I can manage it in the morning. And I'll have you fed and out of his sight before he thinks of wakening,' she promised.

As she went towards the door of the stable Solas turned her head to follow her movements with wide, distressed eyes, like a child pleading silently not to be left alone in the dark, Anna thought. 'Goodnight!' she said again softly.

She put out the lamp and when she had secured the stable door firmly behind her she went back to the house. Just as she was about to go inside a faint whinny was borne on the wind. Solas often gave just one whinny shortly after she had been stabled and normally Anna took it as a noise of appreciation, but tonight she was disturbed by the sound. She paused, listening for the whinny to be repeated. In the lamplight it had been impossible to make a thorough examination of the horse's condition and the worry persisted. How fierce had been the punishment Fergus had inflicted on Solas while he had been on his meat round? How cruel had been his neglect of the mare's needs? There was no further sound of whinnying but, as she stood staring into the darkness, wishing that she was about to enter a less forbidding dwelling and that she herself was not so much in dread of its debauched occupant, there formed the conviction that she was no longer alone in her detestation of Fergus: in the last three days Solas also had learned to fear and hate her husband.

A spell of calm weather caused Fergus to forgo his meat

133

round and resume fishing and Anna, thankful that he was so frequently away from home and that Solas was spared the ignominy of pulling a cart, took advantage of the respite to reflect on her own position. Now that she had the mare to look after she had resolutely to adjust her ideas about leaving Fergus. Her savings were not mounting as quickly as she had hoped but the fact no longer disturbed her. Since she would not consider abandoning Solas to Fergus's pitiless hands she knew she must be prepared to stay until she had found some way of ensuring the horse had a good home. Once again what she thought of as the 'neverness' of her life closed in on her and though she had never ridden a horse there were times when she was assailed by wild dreams of mounting Solas and riding away to the far hills, sleeping rough as she remembered Jimmy Pearl doing and, like him, earning her keep wherever she could. But she would not be able to ride far enough away from Fergus. A man might do such a thing but a woman, being a possession by marriage, would be regarded as a certifiable lunatic were she to attempt it.

Following Fergus's one venture into meat hawking Anna began to notice a difference in Solas. Although the mare did not seem to be losing condition there was about her a kind of languor which not even extra feeding could combat. Worried, she decided to seek advice from her cousin Alistair. Since he had a horse, albeit a much hardier one than Solas, she reckoned he should have sufficient knowledge of horses to tell her what was wrong.

'I don't see much wrong with her at all,' Alistair opined. 'No more than I doubt she's in foal.'

'In foal? How can that be?' the pronouncement staggered Anna.

'I reckon she must have been in foal when Fergus got her,' Alistair said. 'She doesn't look as if she's that far off it now.'

Half excited, half dismayed, Anna looked long at Solas before she turned to Alistair. 'Alistair,' she said, 'you will do me the favour of not mentioning what you have told me to anyone at all.'

He shrugged. 'If that is the way you want it, surely,' he promised.

The calm spell gave way to moderate winds which brought heavy snowfalls. The snow froze and since the cattle had to be housed at night much of Anna's time was spent breaking the ice on the rain-water butts and carrying pails of water to the byre. Fergus came home and announced that fishing was poor and therefore he intended to slaughter more sheep to sell. 'You'd best bring the horse in for the night,' he told Anna.

'The horse is in the stable,' Anna said.

Fergus turned on her. 'I told you to leave the beast out on the hill,' he berated her. 'I'll not . . .'

'The horse is sick, that is why she is in the stable,' Anna interrupted, having judged it best not to tell him the mare was in foal. 'I am warning you, it is too sick to go into harness. It could easily die on you and you would be left stranded.'

He let out a stream of invective against Solas.

'If you are determined to go with the cart I will speak to my cousin Alistair to see if he will give you a lend of his horse,' Anna volunteered.

Fergus grunted.

Alistair argued, 'This is no weather for any horse to be out pulling a cart. It could slip and break its leg.'

'Fergus is determined to go,' she told him. 'And, well you know, the horse we have is not fit.'

'Indeed no,' he agreed. He hesitated for a while. 'I will give Fergus a lend of my horse so long as I go along with him,' he offered. 'I'll not have my beast driven hard nor standing around in the cold.'

'I will give Fergus your message,' she said.

To Anna's great relief Fergus, though not agreeing with

135

alacrity, made no objection to borrowing Alistair's horse and to enduring Alistair's company. Indeed, she formed the impression that he was not averse to having a more experienced horse in the shafts and a more experienced driver to negotiate the tricky conditions they were likely to encounter.

The meat had been jointed, wrapped and left out in the shed ready to be loaded at first light the following morning, and when the day dawned calm and with a hint that it might allow a slight thaw Anna went about her work comforted by the knowledge that her cousin would not go back on his promise. She gave Solas her morning feed but left the mare in the stable to wait until the day warmed up a little before putting her out for exercise. She fed the cows and turned them out onto the croft to scrape for a little food under the snow. She went to the well for water but, finding it frozen, she had to carry on until she reached the spring. When she got back she saw with satisfaction that the cart and the meat had gone. Undoubtedly Alistair had been anxious to make an early start. He would also insist on returning home before dark but she doubted if Fergus would come back with him. Even if he did, she had the prospect of a few hours at least without his scowling presence.

It was about an hour later that she decided the day was mild enough for Solas to be turned out for exercise. Even before she reached the stable she sensed its emptiness. 'No!' she exclaimed. 'Dear God! No!' Still refuting the evidence of her own eyes, she set out for Alistair's croft, slipping and sliding through the snow and ice. She was met by the sight of Alistair's horse feeding beside the fenced haystack from which Alistair was pulling hay.

When he saw her approaching he called out, 'When I got there – and I was in plenty of time – Fergus had the horse in the shafts and was shouting at me that I wasn't wanted.' His face, already flushed with the cold, had the deeper flush of anger. Obviously he was still smarting that his help had been rejected so disdainfully. 'Wasting my time, that's what it was,' he grumbled. His attitude mellowed as he saw her shrink from his acrimony. 'The man must be mad,' he said.

So Fergus had once again proved his treachery! She saw now that he had never had any intention of borrowing Alistair's horse or of having Alistair's company imposed on him. His apparent acceptance of the arrangement had simply been a subterfuge. Her eyes looked emptily into the distance. 'Yes, he is mad,' she admitted and, broken by the knowledge of her own gullibility, she turned and made her way back to the house.

Dusk had spread itself over the sky but the snow-mantled land lent light to the evening. Anna was hammering with a boulder at the thick ice on the water butts so as to get water for the cattle when she heard shouts ringing across the snow. As she listened the shouts resolved themselves into curses and, peering into the dusk, she discerned Fergus leading the snorting, distraught Solas towards the house. Her relief that he had at least brought the mare back in time to be sheltered for the night was offset by seeing him pull the horse to a halt beside one of the posts which held her washing line. She wondered if he intended to leave the mare there ready for her to stable. The next moment she was wondering where he had left the cart. While she continued to fill the pails with lumps of ice ready to take over to the house to thaw she kept an anxious eye on what Fergus was doing. She saw him tie the horse to the post, saw him go over to his creel shed, and, knowing he would be up to no good, she sped towards Solas and began trying to untie the rope that held her. The knot was tight; her fingers were stiff with cold and she was still struggling with the rope when Fergus emerged from the creel shed and crunched heavily through the snow towards her.

'Leave that beast alone!' he bellowed.

As she swung to face him she saw to her horror the heavy

137

horsewhip which he grasped in his hand. She hated the sight of the light whip which had come as part of the tackle when the cart had been delivered but this one was several times more menacing. Since she had never seen it she wondered how it had come into his possession. Was it with this whip that he had inflicted the weals she had found earlier on Solas, she asked herself. She moved towards him, blocking his path. 'No!' she denied him, her voice grating with emphasis. 'No, you shall not use that whip on this horse.'

'Get out of my way!' He raised the whip as if he was about to strike her but she stood squarely in front of him. The whip stayed raised. 'That beast turned the cart over and wrecked it and lost all the meat,' he snarled.

'It would be your own handling of her that caused that,' she accused him. 'And you should not have taken the mare. Didn't I tell you she was sick?'

'Sick! I'll make her sick!' he boasted, and before Anna could do anything to impede him he had brought the whip down across the mare's back. Solas reared and plunged, squealing with pain.

'No!' Anna screamed desperately and tried to hang with her full weight on the arm that held the whip. But she was no match for him. Suddenly thrusting back his elbow, he dug her savagely in the breast, knocking the breath out of her and causing her to fall on her side. But the snow cushioned the impact and, recovering herself quickly, she ran towards the water butts.

'That'll teach you to keep out of my way!' Fergus shouted at her.

But Anna had no thought of keeping out of his way. Grabbing the two pails of broken ice, she ran towards him and as he raised the whip a second time she rushed in and flung the contents of the first pail into his face. He staggered back and for an instant looked as if he could not believe the sudden assault. And then, with a roar of abuse, he came at her, the whip held menacingly. She hurled the second pail at him, and as he jinked to try to avoid its contents his feet slid from under him and he fell heavily on his back, letting go of the horsewhip as he did so. In a flash Anna had darted forward and snatched it, and as Fergus struggled to his feet she raised it threateningly knowing that nothing would stop her from using it should he again try to attack her or Solas. He got to his feet and stood breathing heavily. Grim and determined she stayed poised within striking distance. He wiped a hand over one of his eyes and then looked at his hand distastefully. She saw it was smeared with blood.

'You could have blinded me with that ice,' he charged her truculently.

Certain that his charge was simply a ploy to get her to relax her guard, she tightened her grip on the whip.

'Fergus McFee, I am telling you that if you take one step nearer I will strike you with this whip across your face,' she declaimed in a voice that did not seem to be her own, any more than the burning anger which was shortening her breath and consuming her body seemed to be part of her.

Manifestly bedazed by her unexampled combativeness, Fergus stood staring at her, his legs planted widely apart, his arms hanging loosely at his sides in the attitude of a wrestler contemplating his next move. Anna's gaze opposed him unwaveringly until, without a word, he turned abruptly and shambled back to the house, kicking the door shut behind him.

Unable to believe he was as subdued as he appeared to be, Anna waited for his next move, daring to ask herself meantime whether, now he had seen she was prepared to counter his bullying, he might be less inclined to tyrannize over her or whether, on the other hand, her show of fight would serve to increase his aggression towards her. When some minutes had elapsed with no sign that Fergus was bent on retaliatory action Anna buried the horsewhip under the

139

snow for temporary concealment while she began feverishly to untie the rope which held the distressed Solas. Her efforts were no longer hindered by cold fingers – the fire of her anger still burned in every part of her body – and the knot soon yielded. Once she had stabled the mare Anna quickly retrieved the whip. It would become her weapon, she decided, and it must be within reach ready for whenever she felt threatened.

She was back at the water butts breaking more ice to fill the pails when she saw Fergus, clad in bulky oilskins, emerge from the lamplit doorway of the cottage. Hiding herself behind the wall of the byre, she watched him. She had never known him go fishing so late in the evening and it seemed too good to be true that he should have chosen to do so on this particular evening. Anticipating that it might be the beginning of yet another deceit, she held the horsewhip, rehearsing in her mind her tactics should he approach her and try to wrest the whip from her. With bated breath she listened to his booted feet crunching through the snow; she heard them pass the byre and then recede as he headed for the shore. Some time later there came the unmistakable sound of a boat's engine starting and then droning and fading into the stillness of the night. He was gone. The sense of relief made her feel light-headed. Where and why he had gone out so late at night was of no consequence, though she thought it more likely his purpose was not to go fishing but to make for the mainland harbour where he could be sure of having his wounded vanity consoled by the sensual pleasures available there. It gave Anna a grim pleasure that he had felt the need to do so. He was gone, she rejoiced, and the air felt sweeter for his absence. Not only would she have time to recover from the experience of the past hour but until he returned both she and Solas would be spared the expectation of his sadistic persecution. As she stood leaning against the byre in the frosty moonlight, her feet deep in the snow, she suddenly

140

realized she was sweating as much as if she was standing in the full sun of a summer's day.

The calm of frost and snow was followed by strong winds and thawing rain which soaked the land and turned the earth floors of the outbuildings into quagmires. Anna, anxious to make Solas's stable as dry and warm as she could in readiness for the expected foal, dug a trench to drain away the surplus water and to make cleaning-out easier. She opened up draining trenches in the cattle byre; she dug channels to take away the water that lay around the house. The effort involved tired her but the knowledge that Fergus would be only too glad to have the excuse to stay in the shelter of the harbour ensured the restoration of her strength by long nights of peaceful sleep, though she was careful to ensure that the horsewhip lay hidden under her bed.

It seemed as though winter might be over, but after a week of milder weather the wind keened again, bringing a light covering of snow. The snow came stealthily during the night, escorted by a moaning wind which, lacking the strength to swirl it into drifts, allowed it to spread itself like icing over the land. When it ceased it left the roofs and windows of houses and outbuildings shrouded in white. Anna, deceived by the dimness of the light filtering through her window, woke later than her normal time and had to rush about her chores. With the usual feeling of dread she registered the fact that, since it was calm, there was more than a possibility that Fergus might soon return. But the moment she opened the outer door and saw the large, clearly defined footprints which marred the otherwise unblemished mantle of snow she knew that he had already returned. Her eyes traced the footprints which, as far as she could discern, began where the path from the shore joined the path which led towards the house. But they had not approached the house. As she stepped outside to investigate she saw with a crushing sense of defeat that they carried on towards the stable.

Dashing into her bedroom, she seized the whip and ran towards the stable. The door was open but she heard no sound of movement. She paused. 'Fergus McFee!' she called, 'If you lay one finger on that horse I am ready here with your own whip and I will not hesitate to use it!' There was no response and she moved a few strides nearer, suspecting he was lurking inside ready to ambush her. Again there was no sound save a gentle nicker from Solas. Her heart leaped. She was not too late. Venturing into the open doorway she stood, whip ready to strike. 'Solas!' she exclaimed and almost forgot her caution as she saw not only that Solas appeared to be unharmed but that she was exuding a kind of conspiratorial pride as she turned to nuzzle the gangling new-born foal that was pressing itself against her flank. 'Solas!' There was admiration in Anna's tone. Worried that she could see no sign of Fergus, she looked about her warily. With a jolt she realized he had been there all the time. Horrified, she stared down at him as he lay on his side in the trench behind Solas, his glazed eyes staring unseeingly at the wall. Throwing down the whip, she bent over him and saw first the deep gash just behind the ear and then the blood-matted hair that covered the dent in his skull. Her hand went to her mouth, muffling a rising scream. She straightened and moved back a pace so as to lean against the stall. She wondered how long he had been lying there and tried to puzzle out what had happened. It was then that she saw the gun. It lay diagonally across the trench and, without going any closer, she could see that it was still cocked. But where had Fergus found a gun? She had never seen a gun among his belongings, so where had he acquired it and for what purpose? As she continued to ponder her mind began to clear and answers gradually shaped themselves to supply a picture of the probable sequence of events which had led to her finding Fergus lying in the trench behind Solas.

Fergus had evidently procured the gun for the sole purpose

of shooting Solas. He had then waited until the weather was calm enough for him to bring his boat into the bay, planning that at first light he would go straight to the stable, shoot Solas, and then get away again before Anna was awake, hoping no doubt to give her the added shock of discovering the mare dead in her stall. She conjectured then that the sight of the new-born foal had so surprised him that, in stepping forward to make a closer inspection, he had stumbled unawares into the new drain she had dug during his absence, and that as he had fallen forwards Solas, panic-stricken and protective, had lashed out with her hooves, stunning him before he could rise. Doubtless she had then continued to kick until she judged her tormentor vanquished.

Petrified, Anna continued to stare at the still figure of her husband until Solas lifted her tail and defecated. With a gasp of dismay she bent down and, grasping Fergus's ankles, struggled to drag him out of reach of the mare's heels.

She knew it was all she or anyone else could do for him now.

✢   ✢   ✢   ✢

12

Resolutely Anna closed the door on the memories of her years of enslavement. She was free of Fergus now. No longer need her life be shadowed by his presence. His death and the manner of it had shocked her, but she had felt no sadness. Even the finality of watching his coffin being carried to the burial ground had provoked no moment of regret. She wore the conformist mask of grief expected of her which, though many of her neighbours must have been aware she was not distressed by Fergus's death, gave them the satisfaction of believing that she was distressed by the burden of widowhood. Widowhood meant not only virtual penury but the loss of companionship and help, the absence of a warm body to lie beside on winter nights. Anna, having lived close to penury while Fergus was alive and not having been accustomed to companionship, help and a shared bed, felt in no way disadvantaged. Improper as she knew it to be, she had to admit to herself that her mask of grief concealed a furtive, low-key exultation.

Realizing that it was time she went back to milk and feed the cattle and to bring Solas and her foal in for the night, she stood up and stretched her stiff limbs. She wrestled with the wind to capture her tousled hair and confine it beneath its net and, with the feeling that she had been revivified by her period of reflection, started back to the house.

The ground officer who was responsible for enforcing the rules of the crofts in the village, accompanied by one of the neighbours who had carried out the custom of keeping the nightly vigil with the corpse, were waiting for her.

'We were wondering would you want us to help you get rid of the mare,' the ground officer began apologetically.

'Get rid of her?' Anna repeated. 'Why should I be thinking of getting rid of her? The mare didn't mean to kill Fergus.'

'A horse that's taken a life cannot be allowed to live,' he remonstrated. 'It would not be right for it to go out on the hill where it might kill again.'

The idea of Solas being a horse to be feared struck Anna as being ludicrous. 'She is a gentle, quiet horse,' she reasoned. 'If you must know, Fergus was cruel to her. She was frightened of him and, after all, she was only protecting her foal.'

His expression was unyielding. 'You would need to fence the whole of your croft and keep her there permanently,' he said. 'She cannot be allowed on the hill. Neither her nor her foal.' It was an ultimatum. The other man nodded agreement.

'You know well I have no money to fence in my croft,' she cried, and when they were unmoved by her protest she demanded, 'You are telling me that she has to go away from here? That I must sell her?'

'Who would buy a horse that has killed a man?' they pointed out. 'It would not be right to do such a thing.' Their voices were reproachful. The drift of what they were saying got through to her and, not wanting them to see to what extent their pronouncement had wrung her emotions, she turned away and began replenishing the fire with peats.

'There's a fellow over in the port takes unwanted horses,' the neighbour suggested, trying to be helpful. 'He'd come and take both the mare and the foal and maybe give you a little something for them into the bargain.' Taking her stricken silence for acquiesence, they offered to save her the trouble of making the necessary arrangements and took their leave.

The new strength which the interlude on the hills had given her seemed to have dwindled into helplessness. Even in death Fergus had managed to cheat her of her chance of happiness, she cried inwardly. She dragged herself out to milk the cows. The browbeaten Solas in trying to protect her newborn foal had caused the death of the fiend who had maltreated her and for that the mare must have her own life taken from her. No matter how unjust, the sentence was irremissible.

The following morning a young man arrived and, announcing himself as a clerk from the solicitor's office on the mainland, produced a sheet of paper which he said was Fergus's will. It surprised Anna that Fergus had made a will. It surprised her even more that he had trusted anyone enough to leave it in their possession, but her mind was too numb to be surprised by its contents. The house and croft were left to the son of the cook at a well-known hotel in the port, the son he had more than once boasted to Anna of having fathered. His boat was to be sold and the money put in trust for the same boy until he came of age. The clerk gave her a sympathetic glance before continuing. The animals and any monies, since he had given no specific instructions, would therefore become Anna's property. The clerk advised her that if she was dissatisfied she could contest the will and seemed a little disappointed when she dismissed the idea. She also dismissed the proposal made by the boy's mother and relayed to Anna by the clerk that she should continue to occupy the croft until the boy was twenty-one, which, since he was no more than ten years old now, meant that she would be able to remain there for at least another ten years. She expressed her gratitude for the proposal but she was in no way tempted by it. If it would have helped her to keep Solas and her foal she

146

might have agreed, but now she had not the slightest desire to hold onto the croft. Once Solas had gone she herself would go and when that day came she was determined to sever every connection with the place that had left so many scars on her memory.

The cattle and sheep were easy enough to dispose of. She had always been noted for rearing good healthy stock and her neighbours were eager to buy. The money from the sale, along with what she had managed to save, was, she calculated, enough to pay for her fare and for board and lodging until she could contact her schoolteacher friend and arrange to pay her long-postponed visit.

She was going through her clothes chest, sorting out the few clothes she thought good enough to take with her, when Tina-Willy came to pay her annual call. The old tinker's manner was suitably subdued.

'I'm after hearin' you've lost your man,' she said. Anna nodded. 'An' accident, I believe?'

Anna, convinced that she was already aware of the circumstances of Fergus's death, told her the full story, adding, 'She was always such a quiet horse I would never have expected her to do such a thing even when provoked.'

'Indeed, but there are many unexpected things happen in this life,' the tinker declared profoundly. She attempted no other expression of commiseration. 'And you will be stayin' on here, likely?' she asked later when Anna, having decided she would take only one of the flour sack nightdresses, had chosen the drabbest from the contents of her bundle.

'No, I shall not be staying here at all.' She found that simply saying the words gave her a sense of finality. Would there be a place for her anywhere, she wondered. 'I am going to England,' she found herself asserting. 'I have a friend there who wishes me to go and stay with her.'

Tina-Willy raised her eyebrows. 'You will be getting rid of the cattle and sheep?' she queried.

147

'They're already sold,' Anna told her.

'And the horse and foal?' the tinker pursued.

Anna regretted having been so frank. 'There's a man coming over from the port to collect them on Tuesday week.' The words hurt as she spoke them. 'I myself plan to leave on the following Friday if the weather is calm enough.'

'A man from the port?' Tina-Willy probed. 'Would that be that clown of a fellow that buys old horses for hound meat?'

Anna winced. 'I daresay that's the one,' she allowed, dashing away a tear with the back of her hand.

'Oh, my, my, my,' said the tinker, pretending not to notice. She stood up and shouldered her bundle. 'So I'll likely not be seein' you around these parts again,' she said.

'No, indeed,' Anna responded with decision, 'I shall not be seeing you in these parts again.'

'Indeed, but the Dear knows how much longer I'll be on the road myself,' the old tinker said with a sigh. 'It's a hard life and my old bones will not stand up to it for much longer.'

Anna held out her hand and, a little startled at being treated as an equal, Tina-Willy took it. '*Beannachd leat!*' Anna said warmly.

'*Beannachd leat!*' returned Tina-Willy, adding for good measure, 'And good luck to you!' With a last wave of her free hand she ambled off in the direction of the next croft.

Anna returned to her task of sorting out her clothes chest and when she came to the well-hidden matchbox she opened it and contemplated the pearls. She doubted if she would ever have the means to have them set into a brooch as Jimmy Pearl had suggested when he had given them to her, but perhaps her schoolteacher friend might take a fancy to them if she saw them. It would be nice then, she thought, to be able to offer them to her as a gift in return for her kindness. Since she could not take her clothes chest with her she promised Alistair's wife that she should have it and, when her cousin came over to collect it along with her mother's chair, which she also wished them to have, she brought up the subject of Solas and her foal.

'I was gey fond of that mare, Alistair,' she confessed. 'You will understand I have no wish to see her being taken away.'

'I will see to it,' he promised her.

When Tuesday came she went early to her special cave where she would be out of sight and sound of the road and the croft. When she returned late in the afternoon she could not bring herself to look in at the empty stable.

Alistair and his wife came that night to collect a few of the smaller things she had decided she did not want to leave for strangers; the horn spoons her father had carved; the family Bible from which he so regularly had read; the faded photograph of her two uncles in soldiers' uniform. When they were about to leave Alistair took an envelope out of his pocket. 'The horse man left this for you,' he mumbled.

'You keep it for your trouble,' she told him.

'No, indeed,' he protested. 'It is too much! The man was not mean in his dealings.' He tried to push the envelope into her hand.

'Keep it, Alistair,' she insisted. 'I will do nothing with it but put it at the back of the fire.'

He looked at her disconcertedly for a moment before putting the envelope reluctantly into his pocket. 'You intend going yourself on Friday still?' he asked her.

'If you will be so kind as to ferry me across,' she said. 'I would go sooner if you wish it,' she added. She wanted to go the very next day, but he had already told her he had to make a small repair to his boat before it would be safe to take her across.

'I will take you early Friday morning if the Lord spares me and sends fine weather,' he promised.

Friday morning dawned calm and mild and when Anna closed the door of the cottage for the last time she paused and looked up at the sky, trying to detect a hint of later sunshine. Satisfied, she slung the cord of the handbag she had made from a flour sack dyed with crotal onto her arm and, picking up her suitcase, made her way down to the shore. Some of her neighbours waved and those who were within shouting distance wished her *Beannachd leat*. As lightly as she could she returned their valedictions. Alistair was already beside his dinghy ready to row her out to his motor boat and while she watched the slowly receding shore she let her gaze wander over the village which, in the distant past, had been so dear to her. But the ache she had once felt at the prospect of having to leave it no longer troubled her. Its image was too much interlinked with Fergus for her to want to do anything but stamp it out of her mind. Her aspiration now was to get away from it as quickly as possible.

Alistair, complaining of a sore throat, had little to offer in the way of conversation and since she herself was in no mood for talk the trip was a silent one. When he landed her at the jetty she hugged him warmly, reminding herself that, in his quiet and unobtrusive way, he had been the most supportive of all her kinsfolk. '*Beannachd leat!*' she bade him.

'*Beannachd leat, mho ghaoil!*' he replied. When the boat was a little way out he turned and, seeing her still standing there, waved, a long stretched-arm wave. She waved back similarly, knowing it was unlikely she would ever see him again.

At the road end of the jetty the driver was waiting beside his empty bus. Anna went up to him. 'You will be stopping at the Fourlin train station?' she inquired, and when he affirmed that he would be she asked to be set down there. She thought he glanced at her a little oddly, but since he made no other comment she assumed it was because she was a stranger to him. She climbed aboard and sat down. After some time two ministers boarded the bus and, without glancing at her, began a sotto voce conversation with each other. Some time later a young man, shy to the point of rudeness, flung himself into a front seat. Again they waited until the driver, apparently becoming bored with waiting rather than complying with a schedule, climbed aboard the bus, collected their fares and started the engine.

When they reached the station where Anna had asked to be set down she thought the driver again looked at her oddly as she alighted but, since he again made no comment, she bade him an English 'Goodbye', and, taking her suitcase, went through the entrance and onto the sunlit platform. There was no one else about but, aware that she was much too early for the train, she put her case down on an empty luggage cart and sat down beside it. The tiny station was flanked on both sides by thick coppices of trees between which it seemed to nestle with such tranquillity she thought it must surely resent the intrusion of the noisy train which steamed into its privacy every day except the Sabbath. She was captivated by the trees; so tall and green and graceful, they gave the place a well-dressed look as opposed to the naked appearance of the moors which she had left behind her.

Into the waiting quietness of the afternoon there came the sound of footsteps. At last, another passenger for the train, she thought, but turning round she saw instead a uniformed figure approaching her.

'Excuse me,' he began politely, 'but would you be waiting for something?'

She thought it such a stupid question she was almost tempted to give him a stupid answer. Instead she replied, 'Of course. I am waiting for the train.'

'You will have a long wait,' he informed her genially. 'Today's train has been gone an hour since. There's no other train now until tomorrow.'

'Gone! Are you sure it's gone?' she exclaimed. 'Surely the train is due to leave at half past one and it cannot be that yet.'

'I should be sure, seeing I am the station master,' he

151

reproved her. Gravely he pointed to the clock face above the station entrance. She had noticed the clock when she had arrived but since the hands were then at a quarter to twelve and had not moved since she had assumed it was out of order. 'Isn't that clock telling you the time the train leaves,' he told her. 'The same time as it has left every day since April first and will do until October first.'

'At what time did the train leave before April first?' she asked him, suspecting she could anticipate his answer.

'Two o'clock.' He confirmed her suspicions. 'It changes for the summer. Oh, right enough, if you'd wanted the train before April first you would have been in plenty time.'

Anna was vexed with herself that she had not taken the precaution of checking the time; the station master sounded so cheerfully unsympathetic that she had a desire to shake him. 'Would there be any other means of getting to the town?' she inquired.

'None this day, save walking,' he said.

'How far would that be?'

He pushed back his cap to root into his hair. 'Twenty miles, I reckon. Maybe more.'

Rejecting the idea of walking so far carrying a suitcase and wearing shoes which she had hitherto worn only on the Sabbath and which tended to rub her heels, she asked, 'Do you know of some place where I could get a bed for the night?'

Again he rooted in his hair. 'Charlie who has the bar over there,' he indicated the small hotel that seemed to be part of the station buildings. 'Now his wife would have made up a bed for you if she'd been here but she's off staying with her sister until Saturday.' He seemed to exult in being negative, Anna thought.

'Are there no other houses nearby?' she pressed.

'Not for a mile or so,' he told her with relish. 'There's two of them only and there wouldn't be one of them would have a

152

bed to spare. I reckon they must be packed in as tight as they'll go in each of them.' He regarded her for a few moments and seemed to be on the point of leaving her with her problem, but then he said, 'I'm thinking there's a gentleman there in Charlie's bar has a motor. A grand motor it is to be sure and near as big as a house. And that shiny! Indeed, the like of it hadn't been seen in these parts until he came.'

Anna listened to him with only meagre hopes. There was bound to be some hindrance that would occur to him, she imagined.

'The gentleman came in his motorcar a while before the train left though the Dear knows why, seeing he didn't want to go on the train himself nor send any parcel away. Maybe if you asked him, and seeing his own house lies halfway between here and the town, he would be kind enough to give you a lift that far and then you could manage to walk the rest.'

Anna's spirits rose a little but she said uncertainly, 'I really don't think I could ask a favour of a stranger.'

'Wait you here then and I'll ask him myself,' the station master volunteered. 'He's a nice enough gentleman to talk to and, indeed, I like fine just to see that car running along the road like it was a royal chariot,' he enthused. 'Wait now,' he told her as if he suspected she was so overawed by his description that she might steal away. He trotted off in the direction of the hotel and, a few minutes later, came back almost jumping with pleasure. 'The gentleman will take you,' he announced. 'And aren't you the lucky one to be getting a ride in his fancy car,' he announced. Seeing how hesitant she looked, he added reassuringly, 'He is known as a peaceful driver.'

Anna thanked him and went diffidently out through the station entrance. The car was standing there, its engine running. She caught her breath. She had never imagined a car could look so stately. It was, as the station master had said, 'near as big as a house' and the thought of riding in it filled her with trepidation. A man she took to be the gentleman to whom the station master had referred had his back to her as he opened the door of the car and threw in the starting handle. He turned and saw her. Anna managed to summon a tremulous smile as he came towards her. He held out his hand.

'Anna Matheson, I believe? Or would you prefer that I called you Mistress McFee?'

His greetings gave her such a start that she stared at him with an expression of mingled astonishment and dismay. She had not wished to hear anyone ever again refer to her as Mistress McFee and now to be so addressed by a complete stranger made her feel stupid and exposed. 'You know who I am?' she asked, puzzling as to who he could be. 'I am sorry indeed, but I cannot...'

'James Cameron,' he interrupted. 'Jimmy Pearl, as you once knew me.' She offered her hand and as he took it his eyes smiled down at her. 'And you surely are the nymph of the heather, as I once called you. You remember me now?'

She blushed. 'To be sure I do,' she responded, and then suddenly her throat dried with shyness. She studied his face keenly, trying to fit some feature of the grey-haired man who stood before her into the hazy picture she had retained of the young man she had encountered on the hills so long ago.

He saw her embarrassment and his mouth twisted into a wry grin. 'You haven't changed a great deal, Anna,' he told her. She murmured a denial. 'So you set out this morning thinking you would get to the town by this evening, but you mistook the time the train left and since there is no other way of getting there tonight you are going to graciously permit me to drive you in my motorcar,' he said.

The way he spoke partly cleared the screen of forgetfulness. 'It would be kind of you indeed to take me as far as your own house. The station master seemed to think it would be easy enough for me to walk the rest of the way.'

'I shall not let you walk,' he declared. 'I shall take you all the way into the town and to wherever you wish to go, but it must be on one condition.' She looked at him quickly. 'And that condition is that you agree to our stopping at my house so I can offer you a cup of tea and a bite to eat. You will soon see how civilized I have become over the years.' Anna had neither eaten nor drunk since the early morning and for some time she had been yearning for a cup of tea. 'You have no objection?' he asked.

'I should like very well to see your house and take a cup of tea with you,' she assented, trying not to sound too eager.

'You have luggage?'

'Just the one suitcase,' Anna said, and was turning to go back onto the platform to collect it when he put out a hand to restrain her. '"Man for the fields and woman for the hearth,"' he quoted. 'Here it is men, not women, who are the load carriers. I will get your luggage.' Anxiously she called after him, 'The catch is not safe, I need to keep my finger over it for fear the lid will fly open.' She dreaded the thought that the suitcase might burst open and let him see the shabby clothes it contained.

'All safe and sound,' he said as he placed the suitcase on the back seat. 'Now, you will please come and sit in the car while I have a word with Charlie and the station master.' He opened the door for her and gingerly she climbed into the front seat. 'Now I beg you, do not touch any of those levers or handles you see there or you might find yourself careering away to some place you have no wish to go.'

His warning dragged a smile from her. 'As if I would,' she assured him.

Sitting rigidly in her seat and hardly daring to breathe in case she should set the splendid motorcar in motion, she watched him enter the hotel. He was hardly gone a moment

155

before he was back again. Charlie and the station master stood outside the entrance waving delightedly and Anna, not daring to take her eyes off the road in front and yet trying to look as if riding in such a motorcar was for her no new experience, raised a cautious hand in farewell.

'How does it feel?' Jimmy Pearl asked after a short time.

'Strange,' she shouted, expecting her words to be blown away by the wind that was bustling into the car and causing her to hold onto her hat for fear it would be blown away.

'You might be more comfortable if you took off your hat,' he advised.

'I might be more comfortable but my hair would blow about so much I would look as wild as a tinker woman,' she told him. 'I would feel I was a disgrace to your swanky car.'

'You wouldn't be a disgrace to a royal coach,' he complimented her.

He said no more until they had turned into a narrow but well-kept lane. 'There's my house at the end of this lane,' he pointed out. He stopped the car in front of a small limewashed cottage. 'And now you will be able to exchange your present seat for a more comfortable one.'

'But I found my seat very comfortable,' Anna insisted.

'I think you may have found it more comfortable than you expected it to be but you will find the chairs inside my house even more to your liking. They will have no motor grumbling under the seat when you sit in them. And you will not be afraid they are going to run away with you.'

'I wasn't at all afraid, at least, not after the first minute or two. I admit it felt strange but I soon got over any fear. Indeed, it was not long before I began to enjoy the ride.'

'Good,' he said. 'Now come and enjoy a cup of tea.'

The room into which he ushered her filled Anna with delight. It was still unmistakably a croft kitchen with its wood-lined walls and ceiling but everywhere there were

156

shelves packed with books; there were rugs on the floor and, as he had told her, comfortable chairs which looked so inviting Anna longed to lower herself into one. There was a recess bed but instead of being so evidently a bed it was disguised by a draped cover and by cushions instead of pillows. It put her in mind of the settees which had not so long ago replaced the sofas in the Laird's house. Her glance rested on the fireplace which was built of stone but though there was a trivet and kettle standing beside it she was surprised that there was no evidence of any other cooking implements.

'You don't cook much for yourself?' she inquired.

'Ah, come and see,' he answered, and drew her through to a room which was an obvious addition to the cottage. It was not simply a larder as she had expected it to be but a bright kitchen with a wide window looking onto a garden backed by a coppice of trees. There was a sink with shiny taps and instead of the customary black range there was a cooker, so modern in design as to be almost unrecognizable.

He filled a kettle at the sink and set it on the cooker. 'While I brew the tea perhaps you would like a chance to freshen up,' he suggested and, opening a door that led off from the kitchen, showed her the bathroom. 'You pull that chain when you've finished,' he explained, guessing that she was unused to such modern conveniences.

The day had warmed and they sat outside in the garden to drink their tea. After they had not spoken for a while Anna said, 'I cannot thank you enough for the ride in your motorcar and for inviting me to your beautiful house.'

'You like my home?' he asked her.

'It is all beautiful,' she replied. 'Your car is beautiful too and I must say how lucky I feel that you were near the station. The Dear knows what I should have done.' She looked at him gratefully. 'And how you managed to recognize me so easily I shall never understand.'

He surprised her by saying, 'Oh, but I must confess to having had a pretty good description of you.'

'A description? By whom?'

'By Tina-Willy, of course. Have you not noticed how observant tinkers can be? How they try to register and memorize every little detail of a person's mannerisms or appearance? I suppose they think it will help to ingratiate them with their customers and so lead to more sales.'

'Of course, it would be Tina-Willy,' Anna admitted. 'I had forgotten she sees you as regularly as she sees me.'

'More so,' he said. 'The tinkers have a permanent encampment not far from here. I see them often on their rounds. In fact, it may surprise you to know Tina-Willy has ridden in my motorcar more than anyone else around here.' He chuckled. 'She puts her bundle in the back and sits beside me like the queen she is.'

'I and my mother before me were always pleased to welcome Tina-Willy,' Anna told him. 'She could pester at times but she didn't get cross if you were firm about not buying. Some of the younger ones are not nearly so friendly.'

'She queens it over all the others in the encampment,' he informed her. 'I doubt if there's one of them who doesn't respect her.'

Anna felt a sudden urge to tell him of the old tinker's advice on how to make a man respect a woman. 'D'you know . . .' she began, and then broke off, realizing that it would mean divulging something of what she had suffered at Fergus's hands.

He turned to look at her, his eyebrows raised. 'Yes?' he prompted.

Anna blushed. 'Oh, it was nothing,' she said evasively. He continued studying her and she wished she had bitten back the words before they were uttered.

'She told you how to earn a man's respect, did she not?' As

158

she turned to face him he nodded comprehendingly. 'You were married to a brute, were you not, Anna?'

His tone compelled her to reply. 'Yes,' she admitted. 'But I would sooner not talk about it.' She wondered how much more Tina-Willy might have told him. She said hurriedly, 'I cannot thank you enough for your kindness, but I must be getting on my way if I am to reach the town this night.'

'So soon? I intend to drive you all the way so you still have plenty of time.'

'You forget I have yet to find lodging.'

'No, I hadn't forgotten,' he said. 'But before you go I am determined you shall see something of my croft. Come now!'

She followed him across the garden, along the path which led through the coppice of trees and ended at the gate to a field. He paused, leaning his folded arms on the top of the gate. Anna waited for him to speak, but when he seemed to be ignoring her she observed, 'This looks to be very good grazing land.'

He grunted faint acknowledgement, but as she was about to try to draw him out with more comments he said abruptly, 'Anna, I have something to tell you.' His tone had become so serious all of a sudden that she blinked at him in surprise.

He began, 'Anna, I was not at the station by chance today. I came to look for you.'

'To look for me?' She regarded him incredulously. 'How could you possibly have known I would be there?'

'I didn't know, of course. I could only conjecture. But I will explain. Last Thursday week when I was driving home from the town I saw old Tina-Willy limping along the road towards the encampment. Naturally I gave the poor soul a lift – it seems she had fallen and as a result had been forced to abandon the rest of her round – and since I have sometimes asked her for news of you she now thinks it her duty to acquaint me with whatever she hears about you. On

159

Thursday she was full of news. She told me you were now widowed, your husband having been killed by a horse he had ill-treated. That is perhaps true, is it not?'

Anna nodded obliquely and hoped he would not try to offer sympathy.

He didn't. 'She also told me that as a result you were being compelled against your will to have the horse put down for fear it might attack someone else. That too is true?'

Again Anna nodded. Dear God, she fretted, he has been kind to me so I must not rebuff him for his curiosity, but where is it all leading?

'You were very fond of that horse, were you not, Anna?' he pursued with gentle insistence.

'I was indeed.' Her admission was almost inaudible. 'But I would sooner you did not speak of it.'

'Very well,' he agreed. 'We shall not speak of it. But wait now.'

Putting his fingers between his lips, he whistled and within moments a horse appeared in a distant corner of the field. A second whistle brought the horse walking towards them and only then did Anna perceive the foal trotting close beside its mother. 'Solas!' he called, and, looking down at Anna, who stood staring in wonderment at the horse and foal, he put a comforting hand over one of hers. He felt the tight-clenched fingers. 'Solas!' he called again, and the horse quickened its place. 'They are both tired,' he explained to Anna. 'They have come a long way.'

She could not, would not, look at him. He was no doubt intending to be kind but instead he was being piercingly cruel. He might have a horse of the same name, but introducing her to it was bringing her no comfort. Indeed, it only intensified the hurt.

He opened the gate. 'Come into the field,' he urged, 'and speak to her yourself.'

But she was so stupefied he had to lead her into the field

and even then she could not find her voice. She looked up at him, frantic with disbelief and hope. He nodded affirmation and the mare, recognizing Anna, whinnied and walked proudly and confidently up to her.

'Solas!' Anna cried, leaning her head against the soft neck. 'Solas.' The mare blew its breath gently into her ear.

When Anna turned to ask how he had managed to save Solas he was not there, but a little while later he came out of the house carrying a basin of feed and two apples.

'She'll enjoy these,' he said, 'and then I think she'll probably want to rest again.' He looked at Anna. 'Are you still in a hurry to get to the town?' he asked, and saw her answer in the look she gave him. Taking her arm, he led her back to the house.

'How?' she pleaded. 'Tell me all about it?'

'I will tell you while we prepare a meal,' he replied.

'I cannot stay for a meal,' she countered. 'I will be too late to look for lodgings.'

He gestured towards the recess bed. 'There is that one,' he said. 'My own bed is across the passage. You will not be disturbed by me.'

She followed him through to the kitchen, intent on further protest, but he turned suddenly, startling her by gripping her shoulders. 'I insist that in return for my rescuing Solas you must help me cook a meal, help me eat it, and,' he went on, 'tomorrow morning you must bake some girdle scones for me.' Her emotions were in such a turmoil she could not look at him. He gave her a little shake. 'Anna,' he accused, 'you are still unhappy?'

'No, no,' she was quick to deny, and as she raised her eyes to his, suddenly and unbelievably, the knowledge that it was true thrilled through her.

161

13

The mildness of the day had given way to the chill of evening and Jimmy, as he said she must continue to call him, had lit a fire of wood and peats. After they had finished their meal they sat in their comfortable chairs with a pot of tea on a stool between them. When he reached for his pipe Anna said, 'Jimmy, you haven't told me how you managed to rescue Solas and her foal.'

'Does it matter so long as she and her foal are here safe and sound?'

'I would like to be convinced that I'm not dreaming,' Anna pleaded.

'Very well. Allowing for what information Tina-Willy had given me, there was very little difficulty in arranging it. I simply went straight to the only man in the port who trades in horsemeat and told him what I wanted him to do. I paid him well so I got what I wanted.' He glanced at her.

'I shall always be grateful to you,' Anna said. 'She's not a bad horse at all but kind and gentle. I was unused to horses, but Solas,' she shrugged her shoulders, 'there was just something about her that made me feel different about her.' She covered her face with her hands. 'She didn't mean to kill Fergus, I'm sure of that. She was protecting her foal and Fergus was so cruel to her he'd made her fear and hate him.'

'As he made others fear and hate him?' He spoke quietly.

She withdrew her hands from her face and saw him looking at her. 'Yes,' she confessed. She shuddered. 'I also feared and hated him.' Again she covered her face with her hands and for a while there was silence between them. Composing herself, Anna changed the subject. 'You promised to tell me why you were at the station today. You said it was not by chance.'

'No, that's true. I was there because I wanted to tell you your horse and the foal had not been slaughtered but were with me and would be staying with me so long as you wished it.'

'But you couldn't have known I would be there,' she objected.

'No, of course I couldn't know for sure, but I knew that if you intended to travel to England you would have to go by train from this station. Since Tina-Willy had said that you were determined to leave the moment Solas had been taken away, I was at the station each day to meet the bus which you would have to catch to take you to the train. Now, does that explanation satisfy you?'

'No, because the bus arrived too late for me to catch the train,' she demurred.

'You are much too sceptical,' he said. 'All right, I'll explain. There are two buses each day. One of them arrives in time for the train, the other an hour later. I know just how much attention people living in isolated places pay to time and timetables, so I guessed that if you were not on the early bus it would be because you did not know the time of the train had been altered. So I waited each day for the two buses.' He slanted her a quizzical look. 'When you did come I let you wait so I could get a good look at you.'

'It was lucky for me that you waited,' Anna said. 'But why are you being so kind to me?'

'Why? Because in all my wanderings I never forgot the

163

young lassie with the tawny-gold hair and nimble feet who brought me food when she thought I might be hungry. I vowed that if I could ever do anything to show her how much I appreciated her kindness I would certainly do so.'

'It was such a little thing I did,' she said. 'And now you are making it seem like the story in *Great Expectations*.'

'Indeed, except that I was no convict and you did not discover me in a churchyard.' He rose from his chair and, opening a cupboard in the sideboard, produced a bottle of whisky and two glasses.

'Not for me,' Anna protested as he began pouring out the whisky.

'Come,' he insisted. 'We are going to drink to a rescue, a discovery and a new beginning.' He held up his glass. '*Slainte mhath!*' he wished her.

'*Slainte mhath!*' she replied as she raised her own glass to her lips. 'A discovery? And a new beginning?' she queried.

'Haven't we discovered each other after all these years? Surely that is worth drinking to?'

'And a new beginning?'

'Why, your own new life which you are planning. May the tide of true happiness flow into you and never again ebb.'

'I think I have never been so happy as I am this day,' she acknowledged. 'Even if I am dreaming I shall remember the happiness of the dream.'

'When you wake in the morning you will see you are still in this room and you'll know you haven't been dreaming,' he assured her.

'Am I to stay? Are you sure?' she asked tentatively.

'You are welcome to stay.'

'Then I will stay and gladly,' she said. 'But if I cannot sleep will you allow me to read one of your many books?'

He spread out his hands as if welcoming her to do so. 'You enjoy reading, Anna?'

'I am a passionate reader,' she admitted. 'I had quite a few books myself until...' She hesitated. 'Until a while ago.'

'And you have had to leave them all behind?' he asked.

'No, no,' she denied, wishing she had been more guarded in what she said to him. She blamed it on the whisky. 'No, I lost them.'

'How does one lose books? By lending them, yes, but in a village as small as yours I can't think that books would disappear without trace.' His tone was bantering but there was a sharper edge to his teasing.

'No, indeed!'

He saw the distress his question had caused her but he would not spare her. 'How did you lose all your books, Anna?' he probed mercilessly.

'Let's not speak of it,' she beseeched.

'My dear, wouldn't it be best for you to speak of it? I know you were married to a blackguard and it is natural for you to want to banish the past from your memory, but I believe it will be best done by speaking of it either to someone in whom you have total trust or to a complete stranger whom you may never see again.' She was staring stonily at the fire. 'Do you trust me, Anna? Or do you regard me as the stranger you will never see again?' When she made no reply he said, 'Whichever way you want to think of me, I am here to listen, so let's try swapping our stories, shall we? You tell me what has happened to you since we said goodbye and then I will tell you of my own life. Wouldn't that be a fair exchange?'

She pondered for a little time before she began, reluctantly at first, her voice husky with emotion, but the whisky and his murmured sympathy gradually loosened her tongue. There were points in her story when she could sense his restless anger; moments when she dared not look at him for fear she would be overcome by weeping. When she had told him everything she felt as if she had rid herself of a handicap. 'You were right to persuade me to speak of those times. I wanted to smother the bitterness I felt but I realize smothering would

165

have been no remedy. I needed to tear it out of myself no matter how much it costs me. I believe talking to you has already helped.'

'It is always wiser to talk of one's grief,' he agreed.

He tried to top her glass but she hastily covered it with her hand. 'I am not used to drinking whisky,' she told him. 'I shall become drowsy and before I go to sleep I want to hear what happened to you after you bade me *Beannachd leat* so long ago.'

'Oh, I wandered around a bit. Then I joined up with a fellow I'd met and we emigrated to Australia and started prospecting. We were doing pretty well too, but the war with Germany broke out and, being good patriots, we joined up and came over here. My partner married an English girl and stayed here but I chummed up with a Canadian chap and at the end of the war we agreed we'd set up a store over there. We managed to add three more stores and were doing well, but trade wasn't what I really wanted. He bought me out and I went farming, but times were looking bad so I got out of that and began to learn about motorcars. I reckoned there was going to be a big future for car mechanics.'

'Did you ever marry?' Anna asked.

'Yes, I married, but I made the mistake of marrying a city girl, and when I went farming she didn't take to the life at all. I suppose I was selfish. Anyway I had the misfortune to break my leg and had to go to hospital. She only waited until I was walking again before she told me she was going off with the doctor who'd attended me.'

'That must have made you very sad,' Anna sympathized.

'Oh, I was pretty sore about it for a while, but I had to be honest and admit to myself that I'd seen the break coming. She wanted to go back to city life and I couldn't abide cities.'

'Do you still feel the same about cities as you did when you talked to me on the moors?'

He looked surprised. 'Did I tell you then that I hated cities?'

'You did indeed. It is something I have not forgotten.'

He seemed amused that she had remembered. 'I probably sounded much more emphatic about it then than I do now,' he said. They exchanged smiles.

'Did you ever see your parents again?' she inquired. 'My father said you were estranged.'

'I saw my mother while I was over here during the war. She'd taken to her bed by then and I managed to pay her a short visit. She hadn't really forgiven me, and my father wouldn't even see me.' He gave a rueful sigh.

'Have you no children of your own?'

'No. I've heard that my ex-wife has since had children but she didn't want any when she was married to me.' She heard the edge of resentment in his tone. 'So, now, weary Anna, how much more do you want to know before you go to your bed? You are feeling weary, aren't you?'

She yawned. 'Not so weary that I intend letting you off without finishing your story. I want to know why you came back to Scotland and what you are doing with yourself now you are here?'

'I came because I was beginning to feel an increasing longing to visit the scenes of my childhood and, once here, the idea of living on a croft with the hills at the back of me and my feet on the shore and a town within easy motoring distance was too much of a lure to resist. I reckoned there was an opening for a garage in the town so I bought a site and went ahead. You see, I'd got pretty fond of cars while I was in Canada.'

'You have certainly the most beautiful car I have ever seen,' Anna commented.

He hid a wry smile, suspecting she had seen very few cars. 'My one extravagance,' he admitted. 'And I intend you to see a lot more of it than you have done.' He stood up. 'And now it is high time I brought in your luggage from the car so you can put yourself to bed.' He went outside and because the whisky had jumbled her thoughts she forgot to warn him again to keep his finger on the clasp of her suitcase.

'Anna,' he began apologetically as he came back into the room, 'I fear I forgot what you told me about the clasp and the lid of your suitcase sprang open as I was bringing it from the car.' He was carrying the empty suitcase in one hand and her clothes draped over his other arm. Blushing with shame, she reached for them, but before she could take them from him he drew back his arm. 'Anna, are these the clothes which you have to wear?' He looked at them with distaste.

'I mean to get some new ones as soon as I get to the town,' she hurried to tell him and reached for them again, but he held them away from her.

'My dear,' he said, 'I would very much like you to throw them away.'

'They are the only ones I have until I can get new ones,' she insisted.

He held up the flour sack nightdress. 'You've been reduced to wearing things like this?' he demanded incredulously, and when her expression gave him his answer he went on, 'Tomorrow, Anna, we shall go into the town so you can buy new clothes, but until then I am not going to allow my home to be tainted by garments that scoundrel of a husband considered your due.' Before she had an inkling of what he was about to do he stepped towards the fire and flung the armful of clothes into the flames.

'No!' Anna implored. 'No!' He held her away from the fire. 'You must be mad!' she accused him.

'Forgive me, Anna. But after what I've heard from you the thought of those clothes ever touching your body again makes me mad.'

She was convinced the whisky he had drunk had affected

168

him. 'Jimmy!' she tried to reason with him. 'I have told you I have no other clothes save those I stand up in. One of the nightdresses you have just thrown on the fire was new. I got it from Tina-Willy's bundle only last week. It has never been worn.'

'Women should wear pretty things, not job lots from tinker bundles,' he reproved her. 'Those clothes were a disgrace to any woman, let alone a woman as attractive as you.' His glance swept over her. 'And I may tell you that the clothes you are now wearing make me angry enough to want to strip them off you and add them to the flames.'

She looked away so as not to see the anger blazing in his eyes. And so he should not see the lack of resistance in her own. 'I now have nothing I can wear when I go to bed tonight,' she told him. She looked at him so tragically that he began to laugh.

'You shall have one of my shirts,' he offered cheerfully. Opening the door, he flung her suitcase outside. 'That thing is too shabby to take on your travels,' he said. 'You shall choose from one of mine.' Going to his own bedroom he returned with a shirt. 'My pyjamas will be far too long in the legs for you but a shirt should be just about the right length for a nightdress.' Shyly she took the folded shirt from him. 'And now at last you can get away to your bed, weary Anna. Sleep well.' He opened the door and then paused. 'There is a bolt here,' he indicated. 'If you wish to use it. *Oidhche mhath!*' The door closed behind him.

She sat for some time on the edge of the recess bed, unfolding the shirt and debating whether she had the courage to wear it. When she did undress and pull it over her head it covered her more than adequately, but the very idea of sleeping in a man's shirt made her feel so immodest she lay stiffly, trying to accustom herself to the new sensation. She could hear Jimmy moving about in his room across the passage, comforting sounds that added to her shyness but in

169

no way intimidated her. Pulling the bedclothes up over her shoulders, she watched the fire flames struggling to burn the scorched tatters of her clothes and as she stretched out a hand to dout her candle she knew she was not going to bolt the door.

14

She was up early the next morning and immediately found her way to the field where Solas and her foal were grazing. The mare greeted her but the grass was good and she did not want to take her attention from it for too long. Anna went back to the house where she found Jimmy making porridge.

'Well, how did you sleep?' he asked.

'Like an old dog,' she told him. 'It is a very fine bed.'

'So, today we go into the town,' he reminded her. 'But first, do you still have the pearls I gave you?'

'They are here,' she told him, delving into the crotal bag.

'Then we shall take them to the jeweller today and at last get them set into a brooch for you,' he said.

'It is more than kind of you but surely that will take too long,' she argued. 'I must be away on the next train I can get.'

'There is no point in your going on today's train,' he reminded her. 'Tomorrow is the Sabbath and there are no trains then, so you will find no suitable connection. You would be stranded again and have to look for lodging in some strange place. It is much better that you stay here.'

'I mustn't take advantage of your kindness,' she said.

'You are welcome and it will give us the opportunity to talk about what you want to do with your life. What are your plans, Anna? Apart from visiting your schoolteacher

171

friend, have you considered what you will do next?' She shook her head. 'Have you been in slavery so long that you don't even want to think what is to happen to you?' She appeared to be a little dazed by his question. 'Anna, convince yourself that you have now left slavery behind and try to reassert yourself on life. You must! You must!' There was an underlying vehemence in his tone. 'It is my opinion that you can best do that by staying here, for a while a least, rather than by sharing a home with an elderly spinster schoolteacher who has probably settled into a very staid and ordered pattern of living. You still have half your life before you. You would be a stranger in England. And if this man Hitler carried out his threat of war you would be better employed up here than in England.'

'You think there is going to be another war?'

'I fear so.'

'What could I do here?' she murmured bewilderedly.

'You could consider marrying me.'

He had expected her astonishment. 'Marry you? Of course I could not marry you.' A blush fired her cheeks. 'We are strangers to each other.'

She saw his eyes cloud at her reply. 'Strangers? And yet last night we talked like old friends. No, I cannot think of you as a stranger, Anna. But is that how you think of me?'

'No,' she confessed. 'But it would be foolish of you to think of marrying me.'

'Why so foolish?' His voice was solicitous.

She looked at him steadily. 'I am near forty years old and I have a crippled arm,' she declared. 'I am no good to any man.'

His eyes did not waver. 'You are near forty years old and you have not a crippled arm but just an arm that, like a tender plant, got frosted in infancy and never quite grew as it should,' he said. 'But you have the figure and fine skin of a young woman still and your hair is just as beautiful as I remember it.' He noticed her deepening blush. 'And what of me, Anna? I am nearing fifty-five and though I have a home I have no companion – no "woman for the hearth".'

Getting up, she went to the window and stood with her back to him. 'I will never again be tempted to marry a man just to have a home,' she told him. 'No matter what happens to me I will not do that.'

'God forbid that I should ever marry a woman simply to give her a home!' he exclaimed. 'Oh, no, Anna. I must make that plain. You will remain no virgin if you accept my proposal.'

He came up behind her and slid his arms gently around her. It was the first time in her life she had felt a man's arms around her. Not even her father had permitted himself to be so demonstrative. She found she wanted to lean back against him and yield to his caress but she controlled herself. 'I don't know how to answer you,' she admitted.

He dropped his arms. 'Think about it,' he advised. 'Think about it while you are shopping for clothes and while we visit the jeweller so you can choose which setting you would like for your pearls.' He grinned at her. 'After all these years of keeping they deserve a good setting.'

When they got to the town Jimmy pointed out a small tearoom, suggesting they should meet there after they had completed their separate shopping forays. He thought in about two hours, and Anna was able to take her time looking in shop windows and comparing goods and prices. Eventually, choosing a shop that didn't look too fancy to stock the kind of clothes she wanted, she bought a plain blouse, two serviceable cotton nightdresses and some woven underwear to replace the garments which had been burned. At the time arranged she made her way to the tearoom where Jimmy was already waiting for her. There were no other customers and after the proprietress had brought their tea they were alone. There was a faint smell of whisky on

Jimmy's breath and she thought he seemed a little excited. Suddenly he said, 'I have an important question to ask you, Anna.' She looked at him in dubious inquiry. 'You have refused to marry me, but I want to ask if you will stay with me for a time. A holiday if you like to call it that.'

'Stay with you in your house?' she asked, startled. 'I can't do that. It would be unthinkable!'

'Why not?'

'First, because you are highly respected in these parts and you could easily lose that respect if folks found you were living with a woman you were not married to. Secondly, it is because I am not that kind of woman.'

'But tell me honestly, would you like to stay here with me and with Solas for a time?'

'If you had a wife, yes, I would like that, but I will not share your home just with you.'

'Then let's go today and see the minister and ask him to make us man and wife,' he urged. She interrupted him with a shake of her head but, ignoring her, he continued, 'Please listen to what I am suggesting. It is that we marry to satisfy convention and that you live with me for a trial period – say three months – during which time I would make no demands on you as a wife. You understand what I mean? If at the end of that time you wish to end the arrangement, and the marriage, I swear I will abide by your decision and put no obstacle in your way. If, on the other hand, you can bear to continue sharing my home, it can only be as my wife. I think we could live happily together but the decision would be for you to make.'

'I have never heard of such an improper arrangement,' she retorted prudishly. 'It might be acceptable in Canada where you have been so long but not here.'

His face fell. 'Must Solas and I part with you so soon then?' He held her hand until she was compelled to meet his pleading eyes.

174

She considered for a few moments. 'It is such a reckless thing to do after such a short time of knowing each other,' she acquiesced.

Outside the tearoom he tucked her arm in his and led her to the jewellers where, after a certain amount of persuasion, she chose a setting for her pearls. Just when she thought they were ready to leave the shop he said, to Anna's dismay, 'We may as well get the ring now,' and because she wished the assistant should not suspect her discomposure she submitted to trying on and choosing a wedding ring. They called at the minister's house and arranged that he would marry them the following week and then Jimmy showed her the garage business he had already started to build. 'I shall need a secretary when this gets going,' he said meaningly.

In the car going back to the house he smiled across at her. She had dispensed with her hat and her hair was loose around her shoulders. 'Feeling all right?' he asked.

'I feel rather as if I'd been blown by a violent storm into a foreign land,' she told him.

He gave a low chuckle. 'I'm going to do my best to make your foreign land a haven,' he promised.

After they had eaten their evening meal they went out together to check on Solas and her foal and then wandered around the boundaries of the croft, finishing up by sitting on a heathery crag from which they could look down at the house and the small coppice of trees. 'The trees give your house such a well-mannered look,' she said. 'I think if I ever have a home of my own I should want trees around it.'

'I'd like those trees to be yours as well as mine, Anna,' he said. 'The house and the garden and the croft I want to share with you.' She knew he was waiting for her to make some comment but she would not be drawn.

She was tired after the unaccustomed excitement of the day but, fearing he might misinterpret any hint she might make, she tried desperately not to give way to yawns. At last

175

he said, 'It's time to go back and seek your bed,' and as soon as they reached the house he bade her *Oidhche mhath!* She heard him open the door of his bedroom but in a moment he was back and tapping at her door. 'I bought these while we were in the town today,' he explained, handing her a rustling paper bag. 'I owe them to you for destroying your own.' Again he wished her *Oidhche mhath!* before going back to his room.

Anna gasped as she opened the parcel and saw what it contained. Wrapped between layers of tissue paper were two garments which she recognized as being nightdresses though they were unlike any she had ever owned. These were the kind of garments depicted in only the most glamorous of mail-order catalogues and were made of a fine semi-transparent material with low necklines and with tiny frilled sleeves all trimmed with lace. He surely didn't intend these for her? She could never wear such frivolous things. Never! She indulged in secret laughter as she examined them. They were beautiful, she admitted, but they were entirely unsuitable for a woman like herself. She draped them over a chair close to the bed so she could admire them in the candlelight and then, with only a twinge of regret, put on one of the new plain cotton nightdresses and buttoned it up to the chin. Daringly she unbuttoned the top three buttons. What was it Jimmy had said to her? That he wanted to help her 'reassert herself on life'. Was he intending his present to be her first lesson, she wondered? She stifled a tiny giggle as she took a last sleepy look at the nightdresses before she douted the candle. The next morning she hid them under the mattress.

They had been married for four weeks and, true to his word, Jimmy had not made any approaches to her. Nor had he made any attempt to hurry her into a decision. Their shared life was happy. Each knew that when they returned alone to the house there would be a hail, a smile, a quip or sometimes a compliment to greet them. And yet Anna was uneasy. There were times when she caught Jimmy looking at her with a kind of questioning sadness; times when he appeared to be on the point of holding out his arms to embrace her; times when she would have liked to bring up the subject of their arrangement for more discussion; times when she secretly willed him to try a little more persuasion. But the repression of forty years still gripped her. She thought she would never be able to bring herself to tell him of her decision.

When the jeweller had completed the setting of her brooch Jimmy presented it to her one evening after he returned from inspecting his new garage. She was wearing the new blouse she had bought but when she tried to pin on the brooch he restrained her and presented her with a flat cardboard dress box. 'It's better suited to what's in there,' he told her obscurely. 'Try it on and I'll see you when I come back inside.'

The dress he had given her was made of tobacco-coloured silk with a pale cream collar and cuffs and with pale cream buttons down to the waist. She put it on and then fastened the brooch below the collar.

'Like it?' he asked when he came in.

'The brooch and dress are lovely,' she enthused. 'But you really mustn't waste your money on buying me clothes. I really cannot allow you to do it any more.'

'I don't think of it as being wasted,' he replied. 'Am I not getting an unpaid housekeeper, an excellent and attractive one too?' he chaffed. 'I have something else for you,' he said, giving her a small silver model of a horse.

He was later than usual coming home the next evening and Anna thought she would go up to the crag at the end of the croft from which she had a view of the house and the road. Solas followed her, expecting to be led to a choicer pasture, but when Anna sat down the mare stayed grazing below the

177

crag. Not for the first time, Anna felt swamped with gratitude as she watched the mare and her foal. To her it still seemed like a miracle that Jimmy had managed to rescue Solas. Her mind went back to the day when the mare had first arrived, remembering her initial dismay followed by the sense of rapport she had felt between them and the hope that Solas might be destined to bring a little happiness into her own drab life. And in a singular way Solas had given her the chance of happiness.

She glanced at the ring on her finger. Again she was only a nominal wife but now she was living in a pleasant home where she was surrounded by kindness and tenderness. She knew she no longer wanted to be a wife in name only but it was the manner of telling Jimmy of her decision that was defeating her. She was wearing her new dress and the pearl brooch and she thought of the other presents he had given her: the model horse, the glamorous nightdresses. Glimpsing his car in the distance, she rose and ran back to the house, knowing at last how she was going to make him aware of her decision.

That night, after he had said goodnight and his bedroom door had closed behind him, she gave him only time to undress before retrieving the nightdresses from under her mattress. Trembling with excitement, she chose one of them, slid its silkiness over her bare body and, after giving her hair a final brushing, picked up her candle. Feeling almost wanton, she opened the door into the passage and crept barefoot across to his bedroom. As her hand touched the latch her courage began to fail her and she had to look at her wedding ring before she regained it. Taking a deep, steadying breath, she lifted the latch.

He was sitting up in bed reading by the light of a candle.

'Jimmy!' she whispered.

For a second he seemed stunned to see her standing there, and because she was unaware how revealing was her flimsy nightdress and because she had never before seen sudden desire in a man's eyes, there flashed through her mind the tragic and terrible suspicion that she had blundered.

'Anna!' he said hoarsely. And the next moment he had taken the candlestick from her, his urgent arms had enclosed her and his mouth was against her ear murmuring his longing as he lifted her onto the bed.